The Convent Rose

by

Lynn Shurr

The Roses

The Convent Rose

Cover Art by *R.J. Morris*

The Wild Rose Press, Inc.
PO Box 708
Adams Basin, NY 14410-0708
Visit us at www.thewildrosepress.com

Publishing History
First Yellow Rose Edition, 2014
Print ISBN 978-1-62830-089-5
Digital ISBN 978-1-62830-090-1

The Roses
Published in the United States of America

"Anything else I can bring you?"

She intended to leave, and he wanted to prolong the moment. "How about some company to help me celebrate?"

She seemed puzzled and glanced around as if seeking other patrons who might want to sit at his table. The pass went right over her head. Eve Burns—still an innocent. Go figure.

"I mean, what time do you get off? Maybe we could go on into Lafayette and do some dancin' at one of the clubs."

"Oh! I—ah—don't get off until nine, and I have an early class."

"You still a student?" Bodey figured she had to be thirty-one now, thirty-two in the fall. Now why did he remember that when he had forgotten the names of half the women he'd ever bedded?"

"I teach an art class at the Academy, also riding."

He noticed that flush rising along her cheekbones, same as the time he thought she'd use her crop on him. "Must not pay much," he said.

"Well, no." Her cheeks grew redder.

A spoilsport from a nearby table hissed, "Miss, can we get our check?"

"I have to go."

Eve sprinted to the kitchen and Mama Tyne. She felt safer next to the deep fat fryers and steaming grill than she did near Bodey Landrum.

Other Books by Lynn Shurr

GOALS FOR A SINNER
WISH FOR A SINNER
LOVE LETTER FOR A SINNER
A TRASHY AFFAIR

Dedication

For Elaine Grant,
who writes an excellent cowboy story herself.

But people like us don't deserve true love—
Renee Niles to Bodey Landrum,
Always Yellow Roses by Lynn Shurr

Prologue

Rainbow, Louisiana, 1982

Two teenaged boys with cowboy hats pulled low over their eyes sat slouched in their saddles at the edge of the live oak alley. The parade would begin anytime now. And here came the girls. Ranging in age from six to eighteen, all wore proper attire for English riding: tan jodhpurs, white blouse, tight knee-high boots, and a black velvet hard hat. Each small, feminine hand entwined with a rein. From delicate wrists, riding crops dangled. The young women rode fat ponies and placid geldings or nervous thoroughbreds in accordance with their skill and experience. They sat ramrod straight on tiny English saddles.

"Trot," ordered the chunky nun wearing a practical short veil over her salt and pepper hair as she pressed her heels against the heaving sides of the black mare at the head of the column.

"Here we go, Bodey," Russell Niles whispered lasciviously to his cooler companion. He tilted his old, gray Stetson back to take in a better view.

At the front of the column where the smallest students rode, some of the little girls' bottoms met their saddles with a thwack as their ponies broke spontaneously into a trot without warning. The older riders out on their daily jaunt from Mt. Carmel

1

Academy segued seamlessly into posting position, their thighs pumping, their sweet, young rear ends straining against the stretchy material of their riding pants.

Bodey Landrum grinned. One of the bolder girls, a redhead, turned and smiled as she passed.

"Hey, hey. That's my cousin, Renee. You watch someone else's backside, Bodey, and I do mean it."

"Look at that one on the very end, Rusty. Her ass is like a perfect upside down valentine heart and that long braid down her back is an arrow pointing right at her crack."

"Didn't know you were a poet, Bodey." Rusty took off his hat, exposing rumpled reddish-brown hair, and placed it over his heart. His ear to ear smile seemed to push all the freckles scattered across his cheeks into a line.

"Go on and mock me. I'm cuttin' that one out of the herd. Just watch me."

Bodey set his heels to his paint horse and cantered into a break in the line just in front of his intended quarry. Her small, dappled mare turned aside to avoid a collision, but the young woman soon had her mount straightened out and pointed back toward the line of horses disappearing over the crest of a small hill. The paint blocked the way again and turned the mare so closely Bodey was able to catch the bridle and stop horse and rider in their tracks.

"Let go!" She was going for her crop, no doubt about that.

"Simply wanted to make your acquaintance, miss. I'm Bodey Landrum."

Bodey loosened his grip on the bridle and leaned back in the saddle so his Junior All-Around Rodeo

Cowboy prize buckle caught the sunlight. He tipped his hat and gave Miss Fancy Pants a friendly smile. He stared deeply into her pale gray eyes and noted the blush rising along high cheekbones covered with soft, perfect skin.

Instead of admiring his own fine attributes, the young lady looked down her long, straight, patrician nose at the worn circle the snuff can made in his jeans. He didn't dip. His mother said it was filthy habit. All the guys kept a can in their hip pocket for show, he told his mama. This girl glared at him like he had a lot of filthy habits.

"Sister Inez will be angry. I'm supposed to bring up the rear of the line in case any of the younger girls have trouble with their mounts. It's a position of trust. Please let me pass!"

"In Texas, we call that eatin' dust, honey. Worst job you can have on the trail. I wouldn't be in any hurry to chase after someone who gave me a job like that. Besides, you haven't told me your name."

"There is no dust. It's a perfectly beautiful spring day, and you are ruining it for me, you—you cowboy!"

If it were possible, the girl pulled herself even straighter in the saddle and tried to maneuver her mare around Bodey's cutting horse. The paint headed her off again, this time pushing the dappled horse into the new spring grass lining the bridle path.

"It is a mighty pretty day," Bodey said agreeably.

He removed his black hat with its silver concha band and dusted off the yellow oak pollen filtering from the trees and turning the air around them golden. Bodey ran a hand through his black hair, making sure he didn't have hat head. He tried looking deeply into his chosen's eyes again. His mama said his daddy could seduce a woman just by looking at her with his sparkling blue Irish eyes. She often said he had his daddy's eyes. Putting two and two together, Miss Fancy Pants should be weak in the knees by now.

Her mare stretched a neck toward the lush grass. The rider pulled up the horse's head. Seemed no one was going to have a good time today.

"If you tell me your name, I'll let you pass," he offered.

"Eve Burns. If you are a gentleman, you will let me go."

Well, since she put it that way, he turned his horse aside and reined him in. Sweeping his hat across his chest, Bodey bowed in the saddle. "You're free, Eve Burns, unharmed and untouched by manly hands." He could sling words when he wanted.

The dappled mare took off as if spooked by a rattlesnake. No stately posting now, but Bodey still admired how the thick white-blonde French braid bounced against Eve's backside, the little black bow on its tail flicking up and down like a whip. He walked his mount back to where Rusty waited for a report.

"What did she say? Do you have date?"

"Nope." Bodey formed his free hand into the shape of a gun and pulled the trigger with his thumb. "She shot me down. I did get her name though, Eve Burns."

"That's good. I can call Cousin Renee and get the low down and dirty anytime you want. Right now, I'd like to get back to the party. Those rich dudes your stepfather invites over will tip me for bringing a drink or parking their car. I could use the cash."

One reason why Bodey considered Russell Niles to

be his best friend was that though Russ stood taller and favored big, red quarter horses he never made a man feel small—even after a humiliating failure like the non-seduction of Eve Burns.

The boys turned their mounts toward the two-lane blacktop running in front of the gates to Mount Carmel Academy. Riding away from the exclusive girls' school, they prudently used the underpass beneath the interstate highway a couple of miles away and rode along the access on the other side passing the new subdivision built on Rusty's uncle's land and named Red Horse Acres by a canny realtor. Two iron horse heads, antiqued a rusty red and mounted on brick pillars, guarded the entrance to what were described in the promotional pamphlets as genteel country estates.

Farther down the road, the boys turned in at the open gates of the Three B's Ranch with its glittering gilded insects attached to the wrought iron arch to signify someone grand like Napoleon resided there. At the stable, Rusty's father took their horses and offered to do the rubdown. Ted Niles wasn't much of one for parties and would avoid an appearance at the barbecue as long as he possibly could.

The boys, smelling of horse and male hormones, continued on to the big house sitting on top of one of the small rolling hills making up most of the acreage of the Three B's. The mansion had the requisite white columns across the front, a swimming pool out back, and an artificial pond with gazebo at the bottom of the hill for fishing. Miles of white plank fencing separated the brood mares from the yearlings, the yearlings from the two studs in their private paddocks, and all of the livestock from the grand lawn surrounding the house.

Out by the pool, the party had gotten an early Friday start. The whole, headless pig, split and spread over the coals, still cooked. The porker's head with an apple in its mouth and green grapes replacing the eyes sat collared in fancy purple cabbage leaves as the centerpiece on a nearby table. When the meat was ready, the table would groan under the weight of sides—slaw and beans, garlic bread, and foil-wrapped baked potatoes with a slew of toppings from sour cream to bacon bits.

Sitting on its own table, the long rectangular slab of the birthday cake frosted in white bore the airbrushed design of a cowboy on a bucking bull. Bodey's mother had stuck two thick wax candles formed into a one and an eight in a corner so as not to mar the design. Beneath the deep icing, the cake was sure to be chocolate, her son's favorite.

The boys slumped into a pair of canvas deck chairs close to a chip-and-dip set shaped like the state of Texas. The bowl of eye-watering hot salsa marked the location of Austin. Bodey and Rusty dug into the tortilla chips and barely got a mouthful down before Betsy Barnam caught them. "Go shower and put on something nice, son," she ordered, kissing the top of Bodey's head.

"Aw, Mom, it's my birthday. Let me enjoy it!" Bodey protested, but he got up and moved toward the house.

Rusty Niles stayed seated. Bets wasn't his mother and couldn't order him around. Sometimes though, he missed his own mama so badly he wanted to cry, even so close to turning eighteen himself. Cancer was a terrible way to die, and his daddy had never gotten over

6

watching helplessly as his wife wasted away. He'd lost her just as he'd lost the ranch.

Some emotion must have shown on his face because Bets turned toward her son's friend, ruffled his hair, and said, "You go clean up, too, Rusty, and make yourself useful."

Trying to look like he didn't need mothering, Rusty stroked down the hair she'd mussed and rose slowly before he couldn't help himself and gave Miss Bets a happy smile. "Sure thing, ma'am."

As Rusty sauntered off, Betsy Barnum returned to the bar where Big Ben Barnum worked an industrial strength blender. When the noise of its motor lowered to a hum, Big Ben poured another round of potent margaritas into heavy, thick-stemmed green glasses blown in Mexico. His third wife picked up a drink with an unsalted rim. She loved his margaritas but couldn't abide the salt. Her silver and turquoise jewelry clanked against her black silk shirt as she raised the glass.

"Everything set for the big surprise?" she asked Ben.

"The truck is hidden in the barn. Russ will bring it around. Then, we cut the cake. Nice work getting him to take Bodey over to the Academy to ogle Catholic schoolgirls while we snuck it in."

"Wasn't hard. It's their regular Friday afternoon activity. The boys are ever hopeful of landing a date with those high class ladies."

"Hasn't happened yet."

"Don't think it will."

"Well, I had to learn the hard way myself. I had me two high class wives and a heap of misery until you came along, Bets. There you were right under my nose all the time slinging hash at the diner."

"I was a waitress, not a hash-slinger."

"And you made me happier than a Miss Texas runner-up and a lingerie model put together. Don't know how I missed you before with all that blazin' red hair."

Bets patted her big mop of deep red curls. "Too bad it's mostly dyed now. I guess you just weren't looking in the right direction back then, Ben."

"When I come into the diner complainin' about how I got took for a ride again with my second set of divorce papers in my hands, I glanced up and noticed you for the first time pouring my coffee."

"I said, 'I wouldn't do a good man that way. I'd appreciate him.'"

"And I said, 'Well, honey, let's go to Vegas and get hitched.'"

"I had to find a sitter for Bodey."

Bets sat her drink on the bar and squeezed Big Ben's fleshy hand with her chilled one. Twenty-nine to Big Ben's fifty when they'd married, now she was pushing forty. Ben's hair had thinned and his middle thickened, but they still appreciated each other. Why, hadn't her husband bought this spread when she complained about the dry Texas heat around Dallas making her wrinkles worse? The humid Louisiana air had plumped out her skin like a trip to the sauna.

Of course, Ben had gotten something from the move, too. He'd sold off the Black Angus cattle that came with the place, installed his racehorses in the renovated barns, and bred some more. They were a hop, skip, and a jump from Evangeline Downs and went to the races most every weekend during the season.

The birthday boy reappeared hastily washed and reeking of Brut. Bodey had put on a pale blue dress shirt and casual tan slacks, but he still wore his belt with the rodeo buckle and a pair of expensive alligator boots.

Big Ben looked at his wife of ten years. "Bodey is as fine a son as a man could want, even if he isn't my own flesh and blood."

Already supporting two ex-wives and two demanding high-maintenance daughters, he'd listened to his lawyers about adopting the boy. If his impulsive third marriage failed after he claimed Betsy's son, then he would have another child to support, this one not even a relative. He'd taken their advice for a change, another bad move in his personal life as far as he was concerned. Bodey had turned out to be a fine and natural cowboy who cared more for ranching than for the oil on the land that made Big Ben Barnum rich.

"Come here, son," Big Ben shouted over the heads of his guests, mostly men in oil-related businesses out of Lafayette. Some had brought their wives. Some had brought their bimbos.

Ben gave Bodey a bone-crushing hug. The boy didn't have his massive build or long legs, but he had it all over his old stepfather in looks. Slim-hipped and of medium height, Bodey Landrum's blue eyes, dark hair, and cleft chin attracted women wherever he went, mostly to high school and rodeos for now. A small crescent scar in his cheek received from the tip of a bull's horn was as attractive as a dimple to females. The kid didn't know his own power over the opposite sex yet, preoccupied for the time being with bull and bronc riding, but one day he would come into his own. Big

Ben had made sure Bodey would know what to do when that time came.

Ben released his stepson and clanged a silver fork from the bowl of lime wedges against the side of a margarita glass. "This party is being held in honor of Bodey, Betsy's boy, who turns eighteen today." Regret that he hadn't made the kid his own tinged his voice.

"We don't want to keep Bodey in suspense all night, so we're all going out to the drive for a minute to give him his gift. Afterward, we'll cut the cake and have dessert before dinner—because that's the way life should be lived. Y'all follow me now."

With Bodey wedged between Big Ben, who kept a heavy arm slung over his shoulders, and his mother, who had wrapped her bracelet-laden wrist around his, the family led their company out to the long drive running up to the side of the house. On cue, Rusty Niles put the black Chevy Silverado truck into gear at the foot of the hill and drove it and the matching double horse trailer up to the house. He parked, got out, and threw the keys to Bodey.

"That's one sweet rig," he told his friend with just a tad of envy. "I'll be lucky to get my dad's twelve-year-old Ford truck to drive to college."

Both the truck and the trailer were custom-detailed with gold pin-striping. On the door, the long gold line curved into racing letters spelling out "Bodey." The boy checked out the door in the side of the trailer. It opened into a small room for tack and had a cot that folded out from the rear wall. Then, he fiddled with the dual-speaker radio inside the air-conditioned, leather interior of the cab. Standing on the deep running board, Bodey showed his manners by raising his hands for silence.

"Big Ben has always treated me like his son, and I want to thank him for getting me this fine rig and for not getting me one of those sissy sports cars he gave his daughters."

The group laughed appreciatively and began to wander back to the bar and snacks being served by the hired help. Bodey signaled to his buddy and dangled the keys.

"Want to unhitch the trailer and go for a ride? Maybe we can find some girls and bring 'em back to the party. So far, the only ones here are Ben and Bets' old friends."

"Hold on until you get my gift." Rusty eyed the access road at the foot of the hill.

"No need for a present," Bodey answered hastily, knowing how every cent Rusty earned went into his college fund.

"Didn't cost me a dime. The phone call wasn't even long-distance. And here they come now."

A sharp, red four-seat convertible turned off the access road and passed under the Three B's arch. Filled to bursting with Mount Carmel girls, some still in their uniforms, others dressed for the occasion, the sporty car roared up the hill.

"I called my Cousin Renee about that blonde chick. It seems Cuz was having a sleepover tonight for some of the Academy girls, so I invited them to the party. You know what they say about Catholic girls. Can't wait to do it once they get away from the nuns."

Somehow, seven young women had jammed into the jaunty little car. They waved like a fourteen-armed octopus and shouted to the guys as Renee brought the convertible to a screeching halt. Bodey scanned the group for Miss Fancy Pants. Four bottle blondes, but none of them was her. Oh well, at least this group looked happy to be here.

Rusty signaled to his cousin to park on the grass between a Caddy and a Mercedes. The girls tumbled out, swayed up the rest of the hill, and skirted the new truck and trailer without giving the rig a glance. They moved on to the rear of the house with Bodey and Rusty in the center of their swarm and ran smack into Betsy Barnum.

"It's so nice some of your friends could come," said the cautious mother. "Since y'all are here, please help yourself to some Coke or Dr. Pepper over at the bar. Bodey needs to blow out the candles on his cake. Then, we can get to the food. Renee, I know you, and these girls are…?"

"Courtney, Jennifer, and Kelley," she pointed to three of the blondes. "Julie, Sally, and Noreen, my friends from the Academy."

Renee tossed auburn locks a shade brighter than Rusty's hair. Her freckles were carefully obscured by make-up, and her lips and eyelids smeared with quickly applied cosmetics. She had thrown on a backless sundress and attired four friends of similar size in party clothes probably from her vast closet. The other two still wore their plaid kilts and white blouses.

Renee gushed, "We've heard about the bashes at the Three B's, and we weren't about to miss a minute of this one. Thanks for inviting us."

Knowing full well no invitation had been sent to this somewhat slutty girl, but assuming her son had called them, Betsy Barnum fell back on her own manners. "Nice to meet y'all. Well, go on now and get something to drink. Bodey, the candles are dripping wax on the cake. Blow them out like a good boy."

Courtney and Kelley snickered. Bodey turned red as a Texas sunset, but obediently walked over to the cake and did the birthday routine. The guests clapped. Betsy started cutting the cake, placing little chocolate squares on paper plates.

The schoolgirls, meanwhile, circled the pool. Kelley pointed out the grossness of the pig's head on the table while short, plump Noreen shook her head of dark curls sadly and said, "Poor Piggy," her deep brown eyes filling with tears. The others, heading for the bar, passed without a glance at the table.

Renee put on her most sophisticated air and requested a rum and Coke from the college boy tending the bar. He eyed her up and down, then shrugged and poured the drink. It was private party, and none of his business. The rest of the girls lacked Renee's nerve and settled for diet versions of Dr. Pepper and Sprite. They swooped down on a bowl of spiced pecans and carried it away to a table on the lawn where the flock settled. Renee, seeing Bodey on the loose, waggled a finger at him and he came.

"Say, Bodey, I heard you want to know all about Eve Burns. I can tell you, you are wasting your time on the Princess. She doesn't date, probably wants to be a nun. Besides, she's Daddy's little girl. I invited her to my party tonight, but no, she's going to New Orleans with her father to see a play over the weekend. I'm surprised she isn't here. Her dad is over there talking to Mr. Barnum."

A bluff, blond man nearly Big Ben's size and red in the face from drink, gestured with a long-necked beer bottle to make a point. Ben's voice boomed over the crowd noise. "Yep, I agree about them A-rabs. They're a sneaky bunch. Who knows what they'll do next when it comes to oil prices. But this is a party. Let's forget about the future for a while—eat, drink, and be merry, right!"

"You sure your boy wouldn't rather have Jag or a nice Mercedes roadster?"

"You done sold me two new Cadillacs last year, Dickie, so quit being the salesman. Bodey got what he wanted. The boy plans to do the rodeo circuit when he's not in school. I said to Bets, let him do what he wants, but she is insisting on four years of college for the kid. Hell, I never went to college, and I'm richer than anyone at this party."

"Is that so?" Richard Burns said. "Nice to find oil on your ranch in Texas, though."

"Go on and enjoy the party!" Big Ben slapped him on the shoulder, then turned to pinch up a piece of the steaming pork with a little bit of the shining browned skin attached from a vast platter just set on the table. Ben swallowed the gob of meat and reached for a pitcher of margaritas. He banged on it with a serving fork.

"Listen up folks, one more time! We got another surprise to announce." Big Ben checked to see if his ranch manager had arrived. Trim Ted Niles, cleaned up in a white shirt and wearing a black string tie, had slipped quietly into the party and now sat at a table on the land he'd once owned.

Big Ben beckoned the boys away from the Mount Carmel girls. He put his beefy arms around their shoulders.

"Bodey here, got offered a scholarship from McNeese University where he plans to head up their rodeo team. I tried to talk him into A & M or UT, but he wasn't having none of it." Applause, hoots, and hook 'em horns signs came from the audience.

"I said Big Ben's boy can go anywheres he wants. He don't need a scholarship, but I do know a lad who does, Rusty Niles, a great roper and steer wrestler who would be an asset to your team. Rusty, you and Bodey are going off to college together. Let's give these boys a hip hip hooray!"

Ben Barnam held up Rusty's arm like he'd just won a boxing match. Russell Niles dipped his head so his reddish-brown hair flopped across his eyes.

"Okay, now. Let's eat this here pig before he gets cold and turns to lard. Boys, you go first." Big Ben gave them a friendly shove and lined up in back of Bodey.

The teenagers filled their plates. Bodey headed straight back to the Mount Carmel table where the girls had accumulated a few stray margaritas. Rusty Niles went over to his father seated nearby.

"It's not right. If the scholarship was for Bodey, they shouldn't give it to me."

"Don't be a fool, son. Bodey Landrum doesn't lack for money."

"We'd have money like Uncle Jed if you had gone into real estate and sold off the land for houses like he did instead of giving it away in one piece to Mr. Barnum."

"Big Ben gave me a good price and a promise not to subdivide the ranch. I'm sorry the money had to go to paying off the mortgage and the rest of your mother's medical bills, but that's the way of life. We still get to live here, and I got a good job with Three B's. It don't pay to be too proud, Russ. Pride can ruin a man."

"I'm not proud. I'm ashamed and embarrassed." Rusty left his full plate on the table in front of his dad and stalked off to the barns to brood.

Bodey watched his friend go. He'd heard enough of the conversation over the chatter of the girls to know Rusty needed his support right now. Who cared how they got to college? Going to the same school they could do rodeo together, chase girls, and generally cut loose. He'd point that out to Rusty, cheer him up. He started to rise, but Renee Niles pulled him back to the table. She'd been pouring the margaritas into the empty soda cans just in case Mrs. Barnum came around to check up on the group.

"Anyhow, I said to Eve Burns, how come you didn't get a car last fall for your sixteenth birthday when your daddy owns Burns Luxury Vehicles? She says her daddy drives her to school every day, and that is their time together." Renee lowered her voice as if she were in the confessional. "Her parents are divorced, you know. He still has to pay for her schooling. I don't know why she's such a snob when everyone knows her daddy is the worst kind of womanizer."

"I don't think she's a snob. Eve is just quiet. She likes to paint off by herself and spend time in the stables with the horses. She wants to go to art school, not the convent," dark-eyed Noreen claimed, ending her statement with a hiccup.

"Oh, drink up, Noreen. This is your night. We've all done it except you, and we have two fine cowboys ready to help you out."

"I don't think I can." Noreen put her hand over her lips to suppress the hiccups. "It's a shin—a sin, you know, sex before marriage."

"If Catholic girls never lost their virginity, there wouldn't be so many Catholics in the world. It's like your duty, Noreen. If you won't do it tonight, you're out of the club," Renee bullied.

Noreen downed the contents of her Sprite can as fast as she could. "I'm almost ready. Bodey?"

"Not Bodey. It's his birthday, and he doesn't want some inexperienced little virgin ruining his fun. Let's walk over to the barns, and I'll give Bodey a present he won't forget."

They tried to stroll casually past the cadre of adults, but the drunkest of the girls kept giggling and drawing attention. Mrs. Barnum called out from a table where Mr. Burns showed her a glossy brochure of Jaguars from his newly acquired franchise. "Where you going, Bodey?"

"Ah, just takin' the girls to see the foals out in the pasture. They're real cute."

"Don't be long, you hear?"

Bodey nodded and kept walking. He'd heard about Rusty's cousin. The group crossed the road and headed for the nearest of the barns where a few mares in season were being boarded. Plenty of empty stalls full of clean rice hull bedding stood ready for a romp. As soon as Bodey slid the door open wide enough to slip the two girls through, he found Rusty kicking at a hay bale.

"Hey, Russ. The girls want to give us a present," Bodey announced happily. When he got closer to Rusty his voice dipped, and he whispered, "That Noreen is a virgin. Never had one of those myself."

17

Russell Niles jerked his head up and appeared startled and suddenly shy. His Cousin Renee busily worked out logistics.

"Noreen, you go over and stand by my cousin. The rest of you girls get out and walk down the hill. Pretend to admire the horses. Bodey, you come along with me to the other end of the barn while we find ourselves a comfortable spot. Noreen Courville, you know what you have to do if you want to be part of the Sexy Seven."

Renee led the way to a clean stall near the rear door of the barn. She checked to be sure the walls were high enough for privacy and saw Noreen and Rusty moving into a stall near the front door.

"Good. If anyone gets caught, it will be them. She crooked her finger at Bodey.

"You got condoms, cowboy?"

"Sure. Big Ben told me never to leave home without 'em. There's two in my wallet."

"Here's how this is going to happen. I want my tits and down between my legs rubbed for a good long time before you stick it in, you hear. You may kiss me as much as you want. You put on your own condom, too."

The ground rules laid, Renee unhooked her backless sundress and dropped it to her waist. Two firm young breasts sprang free, the pink nipples already jutting out in anticipation. Bodey clamped his hands down on the boobs and began to rub.

"Not so hard, Bodey!"

"I know what I'm doing! Big Ben took me to a real whorehouse in New Orleans when I turned sixteen, but I had two other girls before that after rodeos and some since."

"Then shut up and do it."

Bodey applied his mouth to Renee's nipples to free up his hands. He let his fingers wander under her dress and strip off her pink bikini pants. He worked with his fingers until she was good and slick and gasping and bending back into the rice hulls. As he knelt between Renee's legs, he unzipped and fumbled a condom from his wallet. Shoot, he should have given one to Rusty. Well, shoot, just shoot.

At the other end of the barn, Noreen sat huddled in a corner of the stall. Her eyes were wide, and her lips quivered. "I've never done this before. I had to get a little bit drunk to do it." A gentle burp passed her lips.

"We haven't done anything yet, Noreen, and you shouldn't let Renee push you into it. She's bossy and mean. Why, we don't have to do anything. We can just say we did."

"Really? No, Renee will want some kind of proof."

Noreen's dark eyes seemed to fill her face, they were so wide. Rusty bet she thought she was fat, but the girl had a nice round figure and a pretty pink and white complexion like the china figurines his mom collected. His dad had broken some with his clumsy attempts to use the vacuum. The rest sat covered with gray dust.

"Give me your panties. I'll get you some proof."

Self-consciously, Noreen removed a pair of pristine white cotton panties from beneath her plaid kilt, taking care that she showed nothing off in the process. Rusty listened for a moment. The moans and grunts from the far end of the barn were loud enough to cover his exit from the stall. He found one of the nervous mares there for breeding, raised her tail and rubbed the crotch of the panties against the horse. He crept back to where Renee watched, her dark eyes peeping over the stall. "Here," he said, offering the panties.

"Oh, yuck! Gross! I can't put these back on!"

"Suit yourself. Here." He wrapped them in a ball and stuffed the wad into the pocket of her blue, parochial girl sweater.

"I can't go back to the party naked down there, Rusty."

"Okay. Let me think. Turn around. Don't look."

Noreen heard the sound of his zipper going down, his pants dropping. She worried that he might have changed his mind completely. A few seconds later, the sounds reversed. The cloth swished upwards. The zipper zinged to the top of a pair of pants.

"Here, wear mine. I put them on clean before I went to the party." He dangled his tighty-whities on one finger.

Noreen took them gratefully, stepped into the leg holes, and pulled the underwear up. The cotton was still warm from his body.

"Rusty Niles, I believe I want to kiss you."

She did. Her lips were plump and tasted of the salt and lime of margaritas taken on the sly. Rusty put his arms around her and prolonged the kiss. Noreen opened her mouth to breathe, and he slipped in just a little tongue. He found his hands moving to the soft breasts under the simple white blouse.

A shout came from the far end of the barn, then an order. "You just keep moving, Bodey Landrum."

Sounding a little out of air, Bodey called, "You need a condom, Rusty?"

"Got my own, thanks!" Russ tried to answer in the same gasping voice. He whispered to Noreen. "Lie

20

down and sort of swirl your head in the rice hulls."

Rusty lowered himself carefully on top of Noreen. If he wasn't careful, he'd embarrass himself. They kissed some more until they heard a shriek from Renee. Russ rolled off of the girl and instructed, "Try to look satiated, will you?"

They lay side by side waiting for Bodey and Renee to put themselves back together. Noreen closed her eyes and breathed through half-open lips. She put a hand behind her head making her rumpled white blouse gap. Rusty could see the swell of one flushed breast. He closed his eyes and tried to relax. Finally, the other couple came clumping toward their stall. He helped Noreen up and was brushing rice hulls from her hair and skirt when Renee looked in.

"Well, how did it go, Noreen?"

"Great, really great. It didn't hurt at all. I think Rusty Niles is the most wonderful boy I've ever known."

Bodey raised his dark eyebrows at Renee. Renee looked at her cousin as if she'd never seen him before. She sniffed. "Coming from a member of the Courville family, I guess that is a compliment for all of us lowly Niles."

Then, Renee said smugly, "Well, I guess Bodey Landrum is the best lover I've ever had, and he's going to be the best bull rider in the whole world."

"Bodey, Bodey Landrum! Some of the guests are leaving. You come out here and say good-bye." Mrs. Barnum's voice came closer and closer to the barn.

Frantically, Rusty Niles brushed Noreen's backside. She tossed her hair trying to remove all the rice hulls. Bodey, though, he just sauntered out meet his mother in the spring twilight as if nothing had happened. He did keep a hand over the place where his championship belt buckle had gone missing—down the front of Renee's dress. Oh well, he could win another one. Renee followed him, her frock looking as if she had slept in it, her hair as full of rice hulls as if she had been showered with confetti.

Bets gave her son a once-over stare along with Renee and the sheepish couple behind them. "I think it's time for your little friends to go home, too."

The boys walked the Mount Carmel girls back to their convertible. Despite Mrs. Barnum watching from a distance, Renee gave Bodey a sizzling good-bye French kiss of some duration. "Happy birthday, cowboy. I hope you enjoyed your present."

"Yes, ma'am, I sure did. We got to get together again some time."

Noreen pecked Rusty's cheek and even that caused him to blush, the curse of the redheaded. "I hope I'll see you again."

"Me, too." Russ ground his boot toe into the grass and concentrated on his action to avoid looking in those beautiful brown eyes.

The convertible packed solid with passengers again, Renee drove away with her clique, the Sexy Seven. Bodey turned to his best friend. "How was she? Nice and tight, I'll bet. Did she cry or did she like it? Man, I should have told you more about pleasing a woman, but I didn't expect us to get lucky tonight, not with all the old folks around."

"I think I'm the lucky one. Noreen is fine. I wish I could see her again, but she's a Courville and I'm a Niles. Romeo and Juliet's families couldn't hate each other more. Still, I think I could fall in love with her. Maybe I'm in love already, it feels so right."

Bodey slapped Rusty on the back a little disappointed that his buddy wasn't more of a kiss-and-tell kind of guy. "Forget about old plays. Come on, a man doesn't fall in love at first fuck. We got years ahead of us, just you and me having a good time on the rodeo circuit. We'll drink hard and screw plenty of women before we settle down. When we do, I'd want a wife like Eve Burns. You know kind of fancy and refined, not easy like Renee. Sorry, I know she's your cousin and a mighty good lay, but you don't marry a girl like that, now do you?"

"I'd marry someone exactly like Noreen as soon as she'd have me."

"Sucker," Bodey said and meant it.

Chapter One

Rainbow, Louisiana
Fifteen Years Later

Who would have thought the great Bodey Landrum would be spending his thirty-third birthday alone? Rich and famous with that segment of the population who followed rodeo, here he sat in a mansion smelling of mildew looking out over an empty swimming pool with cracks in the bottom. Compared to last year's blowout when he treated his friends to thick steaks, all they could drink, and the cowgirl of their choice, this was pretty damn pitiful.

He found retirement hard to take—even if his bum knee and his bad back had been begging him to quit for the last several years. On this damp Louisiana day, all the bones he had broken during his bull riding career ached. A storm was coming for sure. Since his first action upon arriving back at the old Three B's had been to stock the bar from Plato's Liquor and Food Store in Rainbow, a remedy stood ready and available, but a man who drank alone was a sad case, a very sad case.

The avocado green refrigerator in the kitchen still worked. He had stuffed it with milk, bread, butter, beer, cold cuts, eggs, a couple of pounds of hamburger, and an entire flat of Ponchatoula strawberries that looked so red and ripe at the roadside stand, he'd bought too many. Thinking back on his grocery purchases, Bodey decided to eat out.

He hadn't noticed much action in Rainbow on his first trip into town. The convent school still dominated Main Street from behind its iron gates. The mellow brick buildings, lawns, and oaks had the same air of serenity they had always possessed. The female students still wore the ugly blue plaid skirts and white blouses of which he had some fond memories. The graveyard remained as quiet as ever.

Rainbow itself had changed. Peeling white frame cottages were overlaid with pastel siding, pink, pale yellow, and blue. The small front yards running almost to the blacktop blossomed with mixed spring bulbs set in front of new picket fences. Screening had been ripped from the old porches that now held rockers painted to match the siding instead of old car seats and moldy sofas with the stuffing coming out.

Bodey heard the town council had voted to change the spelling of the name to Rainbeaux in order to cash in on the Cajun culture craze. Mayor Plato vetoed the plan and won support by telling the old story about the miraculous founding of the place under the sign of a real rainbow. So instead, the Chamber of Commerce backed writing grants to paint all the houses in a rainbow of colors and clean up the front yards. Evidently, they had gotten the money. Sometimes, being a dirt-poor place helped. Rainbow had weathered the oil bust with hardly a notice and now prospered in a new way.

The ancient Rainbow Café, once a shanty with a crudely painted rainbow on the side and not a place you'd take your mother out to dinner, had been increased in size and yuppified. They'd added a new porch where large parties waiting for tables could sit on cypress benches among the planters of asparagus fern and purple petunias and smoke if they must. Smoking was now banned where once the people not only lit up, but chewed and spit as well. Ja'nae Plato had threatened to fix the place up years ago, and now she'd done it. Bodey just prayed to God the café still served great ribs.

As a single, almost immediately he got an odd-shaped table with only three chairs wedged into a corner. Ja'nae Plato, serving as hostess, had a paler complexion than many of the Cajuns eating in the place. Only in Rainbow would she still be considered black. Bodey wondered why she didn't leave. She had been cordial enough, remembering him not as a rodeo star, but as a friend of her brother's and fellow graduate from the high school in Opelousas, which was nice, he guessed.

That the Rainbow Café even had a hostess he counted as a bad sign. Hope returned when he caught a glimpse of Ja'nae's mama, Leontyne, in the kitchen still supervising the deep fat fryers. He had to say the Platos were equal opportunity employers. Several white waitresses scurried around the place and some dark-skinned people worked in the kitchen and behind the bar. His server brought ice water and a menu. He waved away the specials of the day.

"Tell me if they still have the best pork ribs in Louisiana."

The waitress, a tall blonde with nice, but not enormous tits and a classic, but not knock-me-down beautiful face, gave Bodey the smallest of smiles.

"Yes, sir, they do. Would you like them with a baked potato, stuffed potato, Cajun fries, white rice, brown rice, rice dressing, or baked sweet potato?"

"The stuffed potatoes still have real bacon in them?"

"They do."

"Then, that's what I'll have."

"A garden salad or a melange of steamed broccoli, cauliflower, and carrots?"

"No slaw?"

"Sorry."

"Salad. Ranch dressing."

"May I get you a drink from the bar?"

Her voice had slowed down and almost drawled the last sentence. He could hear an imaginary "cowboy" being added. That's when he remembered he still wore his Stetson. He pulled his stretched-out, booted feet back under the table and hung his hat on the knob of his chair.

"Jack Daniels on the rocks."

She raised her pale eyebrows over big, gray eyes as if to say, "What, not a straight shot?", but the words that came out of her pale pink lips were, "I'll bring that right away, sir."

His waitress was a little stiff for the Landrum taste, but he thought she might be able to loosen up with some help. He had a long evening ahead and needed some entertainment. He watched her move away, hips swaying under a snug, but not tight, black skirt, her long, white-blonde French braid switching back and forth, back and forth, with a black bow on its tail.

No, it couldn't be Miss Fancy Pants. If she was, the mighty had fallen farther than he ever had off a bucking bull. She brought his drink and salad. This had to be her. He studied on the matter a while longer, watching her serve other tables. When his order came, he said impulsively, "It's my birthday."

"Have a good one," she replied, setting down a massive platter of ribs and a large stuffed potato in a side dish. The bread basket followed with a steaming hot pistolette roll and a thick square of Mama Tyne's cornbread. She added a packet of sanitary wet wipes to the accumulation on the table.

"Would you like one of our rib bibs to protect your clothing, sir?" Again, there came that tiny hint of a smile.

"Hell, no!"

She laughed. It was an unexpectedly hearty laugh, and people at adjoining tables turned their heads and smiled, too. Bodey figured she had just earned herself a bigger tip.

"Too sissy for you, cowboy?" she said.

"Damn straight," he answered with an I'll-eat-you-right-up grin.

"Anything else I can bring you?"

She intended to leave, and he wanted to prolong the moment. "How about some company to help me celebrate?"

She seemed puzzled and glanced around as if seeking other patrons who might want to sit at his table. The pass went right over her head. Eve Burns—still an innocent. Go figure.

"I mean, what time do you get off? Maybe we could go on into Lafayette and do some dancin' at one of the clubs."

"Oh! I—ah—don't get off until nine, and I have an

early class."

"You still a student?" Bodey figured she had to be thirty-one now, thirty-two in the fall. Now why did he remember that when he had forgotten the names of half the women he'd ever bedded?"

"I teach an art class at the Academy, also riding."

He noticed that flush rising along her cheekbones, same as the time he thought she'd use her crop on him. "Must not pay much," he said.

"Well, no." Her cheeks grew redder.

A spoilsport from a nearby table hissed, "Miss, can we get our check?"

"I have to go."

Eve sprinted to the kitchen and Mama Tyne. She felt safer next to the deep fat fryers and steaming grill than she did near Bodey Landrum. He'd hit on her once in high school, and she'd frozen up and panicked. Afterward, she'd drawn his picture a dozen times in her sketchbook and made up conversations between them hoping he'd make another attempt. But, Bodey had gone off with Renee Niles who knew how to handle a guy like that and give him what he wanted. Probably by now, Bodey had slept with a hundred women or more. As for her, did one affair in college even count if the man left you? She put a hand over her thudding heart.

As big and stately as the Queen Mary docking, Mama Tyne shifted her attention from the bubbling hot oil to her waitress. "You sick, honey?"

"No, Bodey Landrum is out there. It's his birthday."

"Well, we'll just have to do something about that, won't we?"

****

29

Bodey settled into his dinner, eating slowly, getting sauce under his nails and on the cuff of his shirt. He did not favor dining alone. When he had been on the circuit, someone always wanted to grab some grub no matter what time of the day or night.

He studied the art hung on the walls, nice landscapes with discreet cards tucked in the corners of the frames. Back when, the décor had been neon beer signs and ads for smokes and chewing tobacco. Once, an autographed picture of his early bull riding triumph at the World Championships had hung among other souvenirs over the bar. Now, the shabby newspaper clippings and photos torn from magazines and taped to a chipped mirror badly in need of resilvering had been replaced by a clear, beveled sheet of glass bringing light into the once dark room.

His eyes strayed toward the exit that at one time had been the pathway to a double set of outhouses in the back. Now, this had become the entrance to a gift shop hawking postcards of the Academy in spring, pastel T-shirts bearing the legend "I've been to the End of Rainbow", and what looked like the kind of religious paintings a tourist would smuggle out of Russia. Icons, that's what they were. He didn't care much for religious stuff.

The painting nearest to his table had a nice big sky like at his ranch in Texas, but he could tell the view came from around here because the grass grew greener and the oaks were thicker. He squinted at the price tag, two hundred fifty. He collected western art, and this didn't exactly fit in, but he liked it. Despite what his dealer said was collectible, he didn't buy anything he didn't like. The old house could use some decoration.

He squinted at the signature "Eve Burns." Now, he took a turn smiling.

Eve Burns wasn't the most attentive waitress he'd ever known. His own mama had been better, schmoozing with those truckers for a bigger tip, really friendly. She did check back with him once, and he'd said, "Doing fine" before he caught himself, and she turned away to another table of diners.

At the end of the meal while Eve cleared his plates, he ordered coffee. He guessed he could sip slowly. His Rolex watch said eight p.m. The café probably had nice restrooms now, indoors and everything. He could check that out in a little while, then hang at the bar.

Eve came bearing his coffee in a thick white mug with a rainbow and the name of the café printed on the side. Right behind her marched Ja'nae, her brother Leon, and Mama Tyne holding a small birthday cake with frosting that expanded on the rainbow of colors theme and one thick candle.

"Oh, no! You ain't gonna sing me one of those awful birthday songs now. Y'all sit right down and share this cake with me."

He blew out his candle, remembering his mother for a few seconds, and sliced the cake four ways with a dinner knife. He quickly cut the biggest chunk into half again as he saw Eve start to drift away from the gathering. "You too, sit and help me eat this cake."

"I have tables to clean."

"Sit down, Eve. Dinner crowd's almost gone. Dirty tables can wait. I want to introduce you to our local celebrity, Bodey Landrum. Eve Burns, meet our four times All-around Cowboy and best bull rider of the century!" Mama Tyne gave him a great big hug, crushing him to her cushiony breast. As light-skinned as her daughter, she stood three times as wide. Her gray hair covered with a sleek black wig made her look like a hefty Lena Horne.

"I wanted to say hey earlier, but you looked real busy."

"You always had nice ways when you weren't being a smartass, Bodey."

"That's how my mama taught me."

"How does yo' mama?"

"Died in a car wreck a few years back. Smashed up that little ole Jag Big Ben got talked into buying for her just before the oil bust. She was on her way home from the country club with a few martinis under her belt, I guess. Mama lived to see me make it big though."

"Miss Betsy, she never knew a stranger. So sorry to hear she's gone."

"And Pops, where's he?"

"Passed on from the diabetes last winter. He's wit' the other Platos now up at Mt. Carmel cemetery."

"Sorry to hear it. Best barbecue man in the South."

"So he was. Finally give me his recipes when he knew he wouldn't last, kidneys going, liver going, everything going. You enjoy them ribs? Just like old times, huh?"

"Was. Missed the slaw, though. Hey, Leon, you do any calf ropin' lately?"

"Only thing I do now is taxes. I'm a CPA. I was back in the office doing the books when Ja'nae said we were all coming out to surprise you with a birthday cake. Usually, I'm not here at night, but during tax time, I have to work the café into my schedule." Leon was also light-skinned and trim but already balding like

Pops though he and Bodey were about the same age.

"Least you can do to repay yo' mama for a college education," Mama Tyne joked with her son.

"This place sure has changed." Bodey dug into his slice of cake to show his appreciation, chocolate, his favorite under that rainbow-striped icing.

"Ja'nae's doing. Give a girl a degree in business management, and she manages the business. Got a loan from the gov'ment to fix the place up. We already done paid the Feds back. Now, she workin' on Unc Knobby across the street. She say Rainbow Liquor and Food need a real deli counter, not jus' a hot lunch case, and a bakery department with fresh goods, not jus' Little Debbie cakes and white bread."

"Y'all know I'm right. Rainbow is turning into an artists' colony and attracting the upper classes out this way. And if Pops had laid off the Little Debbies and white bread, he might be here with us now."

"Let go, Ja'nae. You couldn't tell Pops nothing."

In the midst of the reunion, Eve slipped away still holding her fragment of cake in a napkin. She ate her slice quickly and now quietly cleared tables.

"Artist colony, no kiddin'. Why I was admiring that landscape right over there a minute ago. Someone local paint it?" Bodey said a bit on the loud side.

"You can see plain as day by the card, it's our Eve." Mama Tyne gestured toward her hard-working waitress.

Color running up the back of her neck, Eve retreated to the kitchen with a tray of dirty dishes. She swore she could feel Bodey Landrum's eyes watching her backside. She hit the swinging doors too hard, and a mug fell to the floor and shattered. A minute later, the party could see the bottom of a broom sweeping up the mess.

"She a quiet woman, Bodey Landrum, and life done her lots of wrong. You leave her be," Mama Tyne said softly.

"Oh, maybe a little bit of Bodey would be good for Eve," Ja'nae suggested. "All she ever does is teach, paint, ride, and work evenings for us. I can't believe you were playin' her with that pitiful 'alone on my birthday' routine though. As I recall, you had a big thang for Academy girls when you were in high school."

"Most of the time, I was lyin' except for Renee Niles. Renee told me once Eve wanted to be a nun."

"Lives like one, but never was one. Her mama left her with a pile of medical bills for cancer treatments and died anyhow. I keep telling her to fix up and get herself one of those rich men who come to the art openings and buy something just because they think they should," Ja'nae went on. "She'll be fifty before she pays off all that debt."

"Doesn't sell much of her art, then?"

"Every once in a while, but I suspect her supplies and those bills eat up her profit. She does good with the icons when the Academy sponsors a retreat."

"Doesn't her daddy help her out? I heard he used to dote on her."

"Dead, too. His luxury car business went bankrupt in the oil bust. He had no cheap franchises to keep him going, you see," Leon explained. "One day he sailed off in his yacht. They found the Princess Eve capsized, but no sign of Mr. Richard Burns."

"Her mama, people said, was too good or too lazy

to get a job. They lived off the life insurance money left to Eve for a while. Then, turned out Mrs. Burns had that chronic fatigue problem and went right into leukemia. Tough break." Ja'nae shook her head in sympathy.

The restaurant stood empty now. The bartender told two men lingering over drinks that it was closing time. A couple of the kitchen workers came out to say they were leaving, and Eve had gone already.

Bodey got up and stretched. He snagged the card from the picture he had admired, put it in the pocket of his tan leather jacket, and gave hugs to the women and a handshake to Leon. "Great seeing y'all."

"Come back soon, now."

"Oh, I will. Big Ben left me the Three B's. I plan on being here for quite a while."

Stepping from the restaurant, Bodey stopped in the middle of the gravel parking lot to look up at the sky. He thanked heaven Rainbow didn't have enough streetlights and neon to block out the stars. On the horizon, clouds even blacker than the night sky built up for a spring storm. A little night chill was coming down, and moisture already covered the windshield of his truck. He worked the wipers and checked his watch. Only nine-fifteen.

Bodey pulled a phone from his pocket and dialed. "Hey, Russ. Mind if I come over for a while if I bring the beer?"

"I told you earlier Noreen and our little girl are down with something, but if you want to take your chances, sure, come on over. I just got Jesse into bed. We have the place to ourselves."

"Be right over with the brew and some strawberries for the missus. You're a friend, Russ. Thanks."

****

They talked about old times, him and Rusty. They spoke about his kids. Finally, they got to the sticky subject of the fate of the Three B's.

"You plan on selling because I'd like to make a first offer?" Rusty said.

"I know it was your family's land, Russ, but I spent some of the happiest years of my life here, too. Means a lot to me that Big Ben thought to leave the Three B's in my care after he dropped dead at his annual Dallas pig roast last year. Good ole Ben, boozin' and barbecuing right up to the end. Not a bad way to go."

"Nope, not so bad." Rusty didn't say anything more on the subject.

"That's all he left me. His harpy daughters got the rest and will probably sell off everything but the oil rights. I plan to set up my buckin' bull operation right here. Maybe breed some quarter horses. I can let you keep your lease on the lower barn and the pasturage along the frontage road, but I'll need the rest of the space."

"I understand." Russ kept his eyes on the Late Show flickering on the TV screen, the sound muted.

"I want to fix up the house and repair the pool. Your kids are welcome to swim anytime."

"Thanks. That's generous of you." Russ wouldn't look at him.

"Don't be like this, Rusty. Big Ben paid your daddy well to look after the place. I know he leased to you really cheap, besides paying you the same salary Ted got before he married that widow and retired. How's that workin' out?"

"Great. You remember how Mona made my dad

court her for a whole year before they got married in the nuns' chapel—because she was worth it, she said. Now, they ride, hike, travel, plant a big garden, go dancing, and play with each other's grandchildren. You'd never know Dad had a stroke. Mona watches his health like the physical therapist she used to be. I'm happy for him."

"I still want you to manage for me. There will be more work once I get my operation started, so a raise in pay would be comin' along."

Rusty Niles stayed silent.

"Look, I know you think I have everything in the world, but I envy you your family, your dad, your kids, a lovin' wife. I'm havin' a hard time settlin' in after the rodeo life. That's why I came back here where I have a few friends and some happy memories. I need your friendship."

"You got it. Nothing's changed."

"Thanks, I appreciate it."

They sat and drank beer until Rusty began to hint that he had to get up early. Just before Bodey left around one, he turned the conversation to Eve Burns.

"Noreen keep up with her friends from the Academy?"

"Some. The ones she liked."

"How about Eve Burns? I know she's waitressing at the café."

Rusty threw back his head and laughed hard until he remembered the children were asleep and his wife sick. "You old dawg, you! Never forgot the one who wasn't charmed by Bodey Landrum. I remember when she shot you down on the bridle path fifteen years ago today, a highlight of my teen years."

"So was that night in the barn."

"Sure. I met Noreen. You know, we didn't do it that night. We didn't do it till her senior year in college. She wanted to wait for marriage, she said, but five years was just too long a time for both of us."

"I remember all too well. You about drove me nuts mooning over Noreen all the time. Glad you finally got some." No way would he mention that as soon as Rusty and Noreen had sex, the woman got pregnant, and in his opinion, trapped Russ into marriage way too young.

"How's your cousin Renee?"

"Married twice, but she's between men right now. Why don't you give her a call instead of bothering poor Eve?"

I'm lookin' to settle down. I want quality, not quantity."

"Well, Eve is quality. Doesn't say much for my cousin, though."

"I could have married ten like Renee when I was ridin'. Sorry, but it's the truth."

"Okay, then. Eve has a studio and living quarters in a little place she rents from the nuns near where Main Street turns into Courville Road outside of Rainbow. The house has lots of banana trees around it and an old plantation bell out front, a small grove of pecans off to the right. You can't miss it, but don't tell her I told you where she lives. And don't tell my wife either. Shucks, why am I worried? It would be some kind of miracle if you and Eve ever got together."

"Thanks for the vote of confidence, good buddy. I don't plan on ending up old and alone the way Noreen always said I would if I didn't clean up my act."

Bodey left behind the six-pack with three bottles

still remaining because he *had* cleaned up his act a long time ago. Mama Tyne had been right when she'd chewed him out in the past, saying that bull riding and booze didn't mix.

On the way back to the Three B's, the storm overtook his truck. He didn't have far to drive, but he pulled off the road anyhow and sat enjoying the turmoil in the sky. The rain lashed at the windows, and lightning slashed across the sky. Bodey wished he could ride the lightning and spur the black clouds. One of the things he'd been missing since leaving the circuit was a real challenge, but now that he'd met Eve Burns again, retirement didn't seem all that bad.

Chapter Two

Bodey woke earlier than he should have and breakfasted on cereal and fresh strawberries. He walked around the ranch after he showered, ran into Rusty working in the barns, but made no offer to help because he didn't want to smell of cattle and manure today. When a decent hour for phone calls finally arrived, he dialed the number on Eve's card. No answer. He recorded a message saying he wanted to buy a painting and left a number, but no name. He more or less said the same thing in an e-mail using the name Bullrider#12345 and hoped she wouldn't catch on, but he admitted it was kind of obvious.

Finally around noon, he drove over to her place where the banana trees were just starting to sprout from old, dead stumps and the pecan trees waggled the pale, green tails of their flowers. Eve wasn't around, but that didn't stop him from checking out the place and looking in the windows.

Her home was really two old shotgun houses sort of shoved together at a right angle. Tall latticework placed around where they joined created a private entry. Coral honeysuckle twined in and out of the spaces of the laths, and a big cast iron gumbo pot sat in one corner holding a few water lilies and some tiny goldfish that hid when his shadow crossed their domain. Sword fern sprouted around the moist base of the kettle and between the stepping stones that had imprints of oak leaves. Pots of pink begonias saved from the frost lined the porch. Wind chimes tinkled.

Bodey would have said he was enchanted if he ever used words like enchanted. He was also nosey. He peered into the windows of the building that ran north-south and could see straight through to two more windows and a door in the rear because all the intervening walls had been removed. He observed work tables fixed with lights, easels with works in progress, and a sink about where the old kitchen might have been.

He stepped over to the porch of the second building. This one was darker inside. Bodey could make out by the light coming in a far window she had quarters with an office area, small kitchenette and tiny living room all in a row. The space behind the wall that ran down the middle probably housed the bedroom and bath. Smaller than a trailer home, but infinitely more classy like Eve herself.

Bodey sat for a while on the porch in one of the sturdy old chairs that had been painted in swirls of yellow, green, and blue paint, but Eve didn't return. In the end, he left his offering of two pints of the best strawberries from the flat on a little mosaic table. He tucked a note between two of the biggest berries saying how he wanted to buy "Sky and Plains #3" for $500 and how he hoped she liked strawberries because he'd bought too many for a single man to use all alone. There, that said it all. He went back to the ranch to wait.

The day moseyed slowly by for Bodey Landrum. Finally, he saddled up one of the two horses he had brought with him and gone for a long ride. While he gave Rocky a nice rubdown afterward, his cell phone rang. Regardless of the horse dander on his hands, he answered right away.

Eve said, "I called to thank you for the strawberries. I ate an entire pint with powdered sugar and made a mess of myself as soon as I got back from the Academy—but about the painting."

"See, we do have things in common. I love strawberries, and there are more in my fridge. If you want to come over, I can show you some other ways to enjoy them."

Absolute silence ensued on the other end of the line, but she didn't hang up. All right, either Eve didn't know how to flirt or he'd mortally offended her. Or she wanted to sell her painting and then hang up.

"About my painting," she finally said. "The price is $250. I couldn't ask you to pay more."

Okay, she wanted to sell a painting. "If I think it's worth more, why shouldn't I pay more, darlin'?"

"Because I couldn't cheat a poor cowpoke like yourself?"

"Honey, I ain't poor, and I own lots of art."

"Oh, really?" Eve said the words so coolly Bodey knew she envisioned black velvet masterpieces and the kind of voluptuous nudes that hung in your better bordellos.

"I got me a Georgia O'Keeffe with one of them cattle skulls in it. I hope that skull belonged to one of the ancestors of the bulls that threw me. That would give us a connection. Speaking of which, maybe we could go out dancin' after I come by to pay you for the picture." He laid it on thick, but it might work. You never knew with women.

"Careful, your education is showing, Mr. Landrum. I don't dance, really. Clubs make me uncomfortable. They're crowded and smoky and full of drunks and—"

"Fine. What would you feel comfortable doing with me?" His comment met with silence again.

Eve truly wanted to say "nothing." She'd ridden away from him as a schoolgirl, too flustered inside to handle a boy as handsome and self-assured as Bodey Landrum. Last night, she'd enjoyed the light flirtation as long as she thought he hadn't recognized her. Then, she'd fled again in panic. All these years gone by, and she still couldn't imagine being able to hold the interest of a man like Bodey. Now, he waited for an answer. Desperately, she searched her mind for a nice, safe, neutral activity.

She *was* on the Art Walk Committee and had pledged to bring out as many people as she could. "Well, Rainbow is hosting an art walk on Saturday. I don't have to hang my exhibit because most of my things are at the restaurant, but once I've made sure about the refreshments, maybe we could walk around together and see if there is anything else you would like to buy."

"That's two whole days away, darlin'. You sure you don't want to dance?"

"I'm sure. Take it or leave it."

He took it.

****

Bodey checked himself over in his mother's antique cheval glass that he'd found covered with a sheet and shoved in a closet. He guessed the tall mirror might have been too risky to move, and that Bets thought she'd be back in Rainbow sooner, rather than never. His mama had prized the mirror she'd paid a pretty penny for at Mt. Carmel's annual attic sale. She'd claimed she always looked and felt like a new bride when she saw herself in it. Bodey was glad the purchase had given her joy. He'd learned after a while that most possessions did not.

But, he did look fine as a bridegroom himself tonight in his pale gray suit and ostrich skin boots. The gold Rolex on his wrist was the most expensive one he owned, and his bolo tie had a chunk of turquoise the size of some of the knots he'd gotten on his head from riding bulls. Taking a wide-brimmed white Stetson from the closet shelf, Bodey settled it on his head and set out for the art walk.

He wished he had brought the classic Corvette from Texas, but he'd cleaned the truck inside and out. Just like in high school, he'd spent all afternoon washing and polishing his vehicle in preparation for a big date. Going shirtless had perked up his tan, too, and he had been able to keep an eye on the men caulking the cracks in his pool.

Eve insisted they meet downtown where she had been since three, doling out some decent wines the Rainbow Artists' Association had chipped in for and gotten wholesale through Unc Knobby. The Rainbow Cafe had stocked each venue with trays of nibbles, and the small pastries came from the new herbal tea room, the Herbarium, she'd told him.

The picket fences along Main were decked with old-fashioned, multi-colored Christmas bulbs, and the parish had granted a special license for a small display of fireworks at nine. Mama Tyne promised to stay open until midnight if they had enough customers, and the

Herbarium agreed to sell special teas and plain old Mellow Joy coffee throughout the evening.

Parking came at a premium since tasteful signs requested that no one leave their cars along Main Street this evening. Drivers were directed to lots at St. Leo's Catholic Church, the little white-framed Baptist sanctuary, or the Assembly of God hall. The small bank and tiny insurance agency also left their lots open. The parking spaces in front of the two bars and the honky-tonk overflowed already. Bodey parked his truck behind Assembly of God among lower, sleeker vehicles and walked over to the Café.

Bodey found Eve sitting on one of cypress benches next to a stack of maps denoting the various studios and galleries, both permanent and temporary. Two of her larger works sitting on easels framed the doorway, and some of the icons had been moved to the front of the gift shop. Nearby, Rainbow Liquor and Food showed the art of one of the Plato kin who had moved to New Orleans to make a name.

Bodey stood across the street and studied Eve for a minute. She looked great in a simple black dress held up by tiny straps. No more than a quarter inch of cleavage showed, but the jagged hem of her skirt hung several inches above her knees over a nice pair of long legs. Her shoes were a disappointment—low, practical black sandals when stilettos would really make the outfit—but a man couldn't have everything, usually.

He'd never seen her hair unbraided before, and he imagined it would have flowed in a straight, pale, silky sheet down her back if the kinks of the braid had been washed out, but Bodey saw nothing wrong with the curly effect either. He liked variety. Around her neck hung a ring of chunky, smoke-colored stones that looked as if they'd been strung by a child or a hippie. A long, white neck like that should be adorned with pearls, black Tahitian pearls, ropes of them to slip down into her cleavage and over her equally white breasts.

"Beep, beep!" Rusty Niles butted Bodey with the stroller carrying his two-year-old daughter. Noreen walked at his side, and ten-year-old Jesse, the boy who had nearly been born at her college graduation, tagged along behind the others.

"Standing dead still in the road during Art Walk is not allowed. You must stroll, stroll!"

"Looks good for a woman over thirty, don't she?" Bodey asked, still staring at Eve Burns who had gotten up to hand maps to people coming down her side of the street.

"Well, Eve doesn't have much mileage on her," Noreen huffed.

She still retained some of the weight from her second pregnancy, especially in the hips, Bodey noticed. Rusty, bless his heart, didn't seem to care Noreen was no cover girl.

"So, you want to walk along with us, Bodey, before you make a fool out of yourself?"

"I'll have you know I have been invited to stroll with Eve. Her idea."

"Oh, I don't see this working out." Noreen shook her head. "Eve is kind of ethereal, and you're—well..."

"A cowboy?"

"I was going to say earthy."

"You know, Noreen, you married a cowboy, and I know for a fact he's a great husband and father."

"I married a hard-working cattleman, not the King

of the Rodeo."

"Rusty could have been king, or maybe just the prince, if he'd stayed on the circuit with me."

"Heaven forbid that I wanted my man in one piece and not all broken up! Good luck with Eve or rather for Eve, God bless her." Noreen gave her husband the eye to move along since people now parted to get around their obstruction to traffic. Bodey was half way across the street and heading for the pale blonde artist.

"Eve, you look sensational." Bodey clasped both of her hands even though he crushed the map she held in one of them.

"Thank you. It's Ja'nae's dress and a little short on me." Color moved across her cheek bones.

"She loan you the necklace, too?" He was about to make a joke about its crudeness when she answered.

"No, a friend gave it to me. It's smoky quartz. He said the stones matched my eyes."

"I don't see that. Your eyes are much lighter, beautiful, but lighter."

"Evidently, they darken sometimes." The color spread over her face now.

"I'll bet they do. I'd like to see that."

"Let's just walk around a little. Then, I should come back here. People like to talk to the artists. Not much gets sold at an art walk, but sometimes you pick up a commission or customers call you later."

They moved along the Café side of the road, Eve introducing him to various artists as they ducked in and out of the pretty, pastel houses until the town petered out into country. Eve's house stood in the distance. They crossed the street and Eve introduced him to still more artists. The couple paused at a potter's stand to watch children making animals from some kind of bright, plastic clay. A girl about Jesse's age seemed to be supervising and giving artistic suggestions.

A woman in a denim jumper covered by a brown canvas apron worked the potter's wheel. Her hairy ankles showed between the hem of her dress and her Doc Marten shoes. She finished bullying the clay into the form of a pitcher, neatly forming the spout with a thumb and attaching a handle with slip.

"Hi, Eve, how's it going up at the other end of town?" she asked while removing the pitcher from the wheel with a string drawn across its base.

"Good turnout, Stella. At least, my icon note cards are selling. Any sales here?"

"Doing good," a big-boned woman with short, chopped off black hair answered. "Gaea keeps the kids busy so the parents have time to browse. It works. We're nearly out of gumbo bowls, and candlesticks are going well. Check out this new blue glaze Stella is using."

"That's really lovely, June."

"Would you like a pair of those candlesticks?" Bodey reached for his wallet.

"Not necessary, really."

"Don't kill the sale, Eve. Finally, a man with exquisite taste—who's not gay," June said in a stage whisper. "Pick out the ones you want."

"Two of the big, forty-dollar blue ones." Bodey pointed to the pottery he wanted.

"Hang on to him, Eve. Most guys won't go more than twenty for candlesticks, even big ones." June and Stella laughed at some private joke.

As soon as he took the bag with the candlesticks

well wrapped in newspaper, Bodey regretted going for the big ones. They'd be mighty heavy to lug around all night. He slung the sack over one arm as they moved on. Maybe Eve would be impressed by his manly endurance.

"Interesting couple."

"June and Stella are okay. They've been together a long time. Gaea is their daughter. Sometimes, I pity the kid. They tease her in school about having two mothers. At least, she is accepted here in town by the arts crowd."

"I don't even want to know how they got a daughter. Yeah, I remember when most of these houses belonged to old, black folks, the children all gone off to find work elsewhere. Looks better now, but seems strange."

"As the old people died off, a smart contractor bought up the houses, did lots of inside renovations, and still got four times the price for each one. Not too many people want to live this far out, though, so he courted the artists and writers who come here on retreats or to give art lessons on the Academy grounds. Voila, instant art colony. As one of the first artists to live here permanently, it's been nice to have all this creative energy around me. I have good friends here."

"So you gave up wantin' to be a nun?"

"Who told you that?" Eve stopped dead in the street.

"Seeing as how you're walkin' so far away from me, I figured you might still entertain the notion."

"I failed the qualifications to make nun and that left art."

"Tell me how that happened, darlin'. I truly want to

know."

"It's not what you think. My dad's business went bankrupt my senior year at the Academy. Then, he disappeared, supposedly drowned. We had a long hassle getting the insurance company to pay up. The nuns gave me a scholarship to finish out the year at Mt. Carmel, but there was no money for college. Dad's creditors took everything. Mother lived off her alimony and her friends, had no job, no medical insurance after Daddy died."

Eve broke her narrative for a minute as they walked along, Bodey moving ever closer to her side. "I think most of the girls who go to school here think about becoming nuns at some time or other. After my father died, I suddenly found I had a vocation. When I told Sr. Helen who taught me art that I wanted to join her order, she said the convent was not a place to hide from problems. I should go on to higher education, hone my talents, and then if I still felt that I had a vocation, she would assist me. Sr. Helen got me a scholarship to the Houston School of Art. I took out student loans, waitressed for other expenses. Then, Mother got sick. She sold the big house in Lafayette and rented an apartment in Houston to be near MD Anderson hospital for her treatments. She insisted I move in with her to save money."

"That sort of puts the kibosh on any kind of social life," Bodey said, sympathetically steering her in the direction he wanted to go.

"Tell me about it. There was this guy."

"Knew it." He placed his arm lightly around Eve's waist. So deep in the past, she hardly noticed.

"Evan Adams, tall, dark, and talented. For a while,

they called us Adams and Eve around campus. We were always together. I thought we were in love. He was a year older, wanted to graduate and move to the West Coast where his style of art would be more appreciated."

"Let me guess—abstracts."

"And moving metal installations based on his art. Really, he had a great deal of talent. I had a dying mother and a ton of debt. He moved. I stayed. After Mother passed away, I came back here where I was happiest. I set up my studio. I teach art and riding. I wait tables. I work on the debts."

"No more urges to become a nun?" He tightened his grip on her waist just a little. He didn't want to spook her.

"I couldn't exactly offer up my virginity any more, now could I?"

"But I'll bet you're chaste. You ooze chastity."

"I believe in being honest right at the beginning of a relationship. Poor men faint and rich men run when they know I need money."

"I'm thinkin' you don't do it right. Lots of rich men would pay off your debts for—"

"Yes, that's another one of my problems."

"We all got problems, honey. Another thing we have in common, we're both alone in the world now."

"Ja'nae told me. I feel badly about your mother. I think my dad sold her that Jaguar just before he went under."

"The oil bust took a lot of businesses down. Big Ben cut his losses, got rid of his racehorses, moved back to Texas, and lived off his stocks for a while. He said oil would come back, and it did, but there is no sense in your feelin' bad about my mama. Your dad didn't force her to have a three martini lunch at the club with her friends, then try to pass a cattle truck on a curve on her way home. She went into the other lane, swung wide, and barely missed a van full of kids. She was going ninety when she hit the culvert. Instant death."

Eve's arm moved around his waist. They bumped hips as she gave him an understanding squeeze. With all the talk, they had skipped most of the remaining exhibits and ended up at the end of the street where the Academy grounds began. Eve dropped her arm and started to pull away.

"I should get back to the café now. The buyers might be lining up without my knowing it." She gave a self-deprecating laugh.

"Sure, we need to go back and put a red dot on that landscape I want."

"You know about red dots?"

"I told you I buy art. It means sold." He kept his arm just where it was and turned back toward the Rainbow Café.

"Would you look at what's up ahead?" Bodey said to distract her from moving aside.

Two men, arm in arm, wearing cream-colored suits and straw hats, sauntered down Main Street. With matching walking sticks, they pointed out works of art. Evidently, their remarks were amusing because they laughed at each other's wit.

"Gives a whole new meaning to the word Rainbow, don't it?" Bodey whispered.

Eve tried not to smile. "That's Archie and Roger from Lafayette. They come to make fun of the boondock artists, as they call us. Archie does sculptures that always look like phallic symbols to me, and Roger paints naked men in acrylics."

"Figures." Bodey and Eve passed the couple. Eve gave them a friendly wave. Bodey studied Archie's florid face and round form, Roger's trimmed mustache and shaped eyebrows. He nodded and kept moving.

"They give me the willies more than the lesbians at the other end of the street. Lesbians I can understand. Who wouldn't want to do it with a woman—but them!"

"Oh, don't be so homophobic, cowboy."

"Believe me it has nothing to do with being a cowboy."

They arrived at the café, and Eve went to get the red dot from the gift shop at Bodey's urging. He sat at a table nearby to write out a check. Archie and Roger floated in and moved from picture to picture.

As they passed Bodey, he overheard Archie say, "Poor Eve, still doing her little landscapes. She really should move on and try something new."

"You know I promised Mama one of her icons for a birthday gift. She wants a Virgin and Child. I might as well get it tonight. The checkbook, Archie," Roger commanded as he held out a hand.

"Why do people want icons? They are so stiff, so identical. They leave no room for artistic expression. Your naked Angel Gabriel is so much more expressive. Now that was a form to be worshiped!" The two men twittered.

Bodey stood as Eve came forward to place the red dot. "Here you go—a check for five hundred dollars. The way you done that sky just takes me home. It's worth the extra."

Lynn Shurr

"I told you two-fifty. If you want to pay more, the one over there would make a nice complement. They depict sunrise and sunset over the same location. Or I could paint something to order," Eve insisted.

"Oh, take the money from this luscious man, dear," Roger chimed in. "I'd so like to paint your friend, Eve."

Roger held out a moist, long-fingered hand. Bodey shook it briefly, then folded his arms across his chest.

"Great scar." Roger fingered the small crescent in Bodey's cheek and drew a fingernail down to the cleft in his chin. "Nice chin and wonderful hint of five o'clock shadow. I'll bet you have interesting scars in other places."

He stared at Bodey's crotch. In Texas, Bodey would have hit the man by now, but Eve was watching his reaction. He didn't want to be homophobic in front of Eve who probably had lots of queer friends.

Instead, he stepped back a little behind Eve. "Too late, Eve is going to paint me for the rest of that five-hundred dollars, and I might even take some lessons from her since I admire her technique so much."

"Well, if you ever change your mind—my card." Roger placed it in his hand. "And this is for you, Eve, a check. Archie and I will pick out one of the smaller icons for my mother. Come, Archie." They walked off grandly twirling their canes.

Looking at the two checks, Eve said, "Between this and the sale of ten packs of note cards, I've made my rent and have some to spare. It's been a good evening. Want to watch the fireworks before we go our separate ways?"

"Nothin' I'd enjoy more than doing fireworks with you. But why separate?"

"It's late. I'm tired."

"Used that one before, darlin'. How about I'm nervous and scared?"

"Are you? I wouldn't have thought a man of your overwhelming masculinity would be nervous or scared."

"So, you noticed my overwhelming masculinity, did you?"

They arrived at the barricades set across an empty lot where a crowd gathered in the twilight. A person who appeared to be June of the pottery stand, ran with a lighter down a row of rather ordinary fireworks that could be purchased at any roadside stand around the Fourth of July, but set off all together, they made a nice display. As soon as one row finished, another row began. This might have been the middle of March and not Independence Day, but the audience oohed and aahed just the same.

In the sudden silence when the fireworks ended making the night seem twice as dark, Bodey took off his hat, swept an arm around Eve and gave her a kiss he hoped made her toes tingle because he sure felt it at the base of his groin. The moment was perfect until someone goosed his rear, and he smacked his body against Eve's thin dress. No doubt she felt the length of his longing.

"Sorry, that wasn't intentional. I think Roger pinched me."

Eve laughed hard into his chest and said, "No problem." When she caught her breath, she did suggest he pick up his painting and head home. She needed to douse the fireworks Bodey Landrum had kindled in her own nether parts alone.

"I think the wild and wooly world of art is too much for you, cowboy."

"No way. I need something to do in my retirement. I might as well take up paintin'. What do you charge to teach?"

"I have a group class Monday mornings at my studio, two hours for twenty dollars. But, fair warning, there isn't a woman in the class under fifty, and they can get kind of raunchy at times. They may ask you to pose for them."

"I'd be wantin' private lessons, then."

"That would be forty dollars, and we'll have to work out a time if you sincerely want to try and this isn't some kind of cheap come-on."

"I wouldn't say cheap—with the cost of paint and all. Of course, I'd be willin' to model for you. I'm not as pretty as I used to be. I do have some scars, though I don't know if you'd say they were interestin'. Broke my nose twice."

Eve looked closely at his face as they passed under a streetlight. "You must have a good surgeon. I really can't tell."

"Let's just say, it used to be prettier, and I'm told I snore kind of loud."

"Thanks for the information."

They turned in at the Café where many of the walkers had chosen to rest with a cup of coffee and a slice of pecan pie or a slab of bread pudding in front of them. Eve found a notepad, sat down, and began writing.

"What's that?" Bodey asked.

"A basic supply list and the names of several stores in Lafayette likely to carry the items. Are you an early riser?

"I can be."

"I could take you at eight on Tuesdays before my other private student and my class at the Academy."

"Darlin', that's two days away. Can't we start tonight?"

"You don't have your supplies."

"Between the two of us, I think we'd be well supplied."

"Go home, Bodey." Eve folded the list, tucked it in his coat pocket, removed his purchased landscape from the wall, and handed it to him.

Bodey gave her the sack containing the candlesticks. "Consider these a gift."

"Accepted. I love Stella's work. I'll see you Tuesday. Be ready to paint."

She walked him to the door, so intent on moving him out that they collided with two tall men coming in. One wore a well-cut business suit with a red tie and western accessories. The other dressed entirely in black.

"Just the gal I was looking for." The businessman with the lizard-skin boots and Stetson gave Eve a great big hug.

Bodey kept an eye on the man's hands, making sure they weren't feeling Eve up for underwear. He was fairly sure she wasn't wearing a bra from the clench at the fireworks, but the large man's greeting stayed brief. No need to defend Eve's honor yet.

Evidently someone who knew her well, the guy charged right into the conversation. "Eve is the mastermind of this event, Evan. I especially like the way you put Ulie Boudreaux, the wildlife carver, in front of the bait, tackle, and gun shop. Having the fireworks brought out the families. Nice touch having a place the kids could play with clay."

"Those last two ideas belong to Stella and June. It was a group effort."

"Whatever you say, but I know the truth." He wagged a thick finger covered to the knuckle with a gold nugget ring at Eve. "Let me introduce you to Evan Adams, the artist who is going to do an installment in front of my new office building in Lafayette. It's called *Progress*. Saw the piece in San Francisco and asked him to bring it out here. Might make it permanent since this sculpture really said 'Courville Construction Company' to me."

The man in artist's black said, "That's an installation, Hardy, and Eve and I…"

"Have met," Eve said faintly.

Evan took the tips of Eve's slim, white hands and kissed the air just above her short, unpolished fingernails. He rose slowly out of the bow, never taking his dark, liquid eyes off of hers. "I always knew we'd meet again, some time, some place."

Damn! Now why hadn't he thought of that line instead of flirting with her like any old waitress? Bodey could have kicked himself. The man had a good four inches on him, a mane of dark hair like an untamed stallion, tight black pants, a black silk turtleneck, and ebony Italian loafers. If Bodey hadn't known his history, he would have assumed Evan Adams was just another artistic pansy, which in this case would have been good news. Bodey stepped closer to Eve and, shifting his painting to the other arm, embraced her shoulders. She looked like she might faint, and he didn't want her hitting the floor in front of all these folks, especially in that short skirt.

The other man in western wear greeted Bodey. "Hardy Courville. My friends call me Red. Rainbow is one of my development projects. I fixed up these old cypress shacks, replaced all the rotting gingerbread, and gave them some landscaping thinking people would love to move out of the city to a quaint town like this. Besides, one of my sisters renovated the old family place down the road for a bed and breakfast and reception center, and who wants to drive by a depressing row of shanties on their way to a wedding? Couldn't sell a one until Eve suggested I could rent or sell them to artists for a modest profit. Hell, it was better than no profit at all. And you are?"

Red held out his beefy hand, then dropped it. He tipped his business Stetson back on his head, rocked in his lizard-skin boots, and said, "Why damn, you're Bodey Landrum, five times World Champion Bull Rider and four times All-around Cowboy. Pleasure to meet you!"

Bodey had to release Eve to meet Red's firm and enthusiastic shake. "You follow rodeo, Mr. Courville?"

"I do. Love it almost as much as the LSU Tigers. When a rodeo comes to town, there is always a Courville Construction Company banner hanging on the railings."

"The Rodeo Association appreciates that, sir."

"Evan and I were just about to get some coffee or a drink. You and Eve come join us."

Hardy Courville swept them on a giant wave of hospitality toward an unoccupied table with Ja'nae Plato being drawn along behind bearing menus. Making it clear he was paying for everyone, Hardy ordered a scotch on the rocks and a large order of onion rings. Bodey settled on a beer. Eve requested herbal tea. The sculptor of *Progress* asked if espresso was available and sighed when one of the Rainbow's older waitresses brought two pots of Community Coffee and asked if he wanted "Leaded or unleaded."

Evan did accept one of the giant onion rings fried in a batter so light and flaky it tasted heavenly to anyone not on cholesterol-lowering drugs, but only because Hardy urged it on him. Bodey thought the artist ate the appetizer as if it were a giant slug, but then he had Evan figured as a snail eater. Eve passed entirely on the onions, letting Red and Bodey finish them off.

While Red monopolized his attention with rodeo and home renovation talk, Bodey tried to keep an ear out for Evan and Eve's low-toned conversation. The good news was that Evan had come in Red's car and stayed at the Courville house in Lafayette. They had to leave together. When that moment came, Bodey shook the artist's soft hand a little harder than necessary and insincerely told the man what a pleasure it had been to meet him. He had no choice but to watch as Evan clasped Eve's hand with both of his and promised they would "get together soon."

No way in hell would Bodey let that happen.

Chapter Three

Sunday afternoon, Eve turned down an invitation to go riding with Bodey. She said she had to work on a large landscape for the lobby of Red Courville's new building. Bodey guessed he believed her. He drove past her place both Sunday and Monday nights late and saw only Eve's old white Toyota parked out front. The rest of his time, he spent getting some of the ranch's furniture out of storage and setting up a new computer on Big Ben's mahogany desk. He researched the bloodlines of some cows he wanted to purchase and breed to the meanest fuckers that ever threw him.

Monday afternoon, he made a special trip to Hobby Lobby to get his art supplies. Looking as out of place as a cowboy in a luxury spa, he wandered among the stretched canvases and a hundred of varieties of paints and brushes, clutching his list and completely lost. Two cute college girls a little too young for him and a grandmother, who said he had the most beautiful blue eyes, helped him with the search. All three gave him phone numbers in case he needed more advice.

Tuesday morning, Bodey got up early, shaved, and put on old jeans and a T-shirt with holes in it because he imagined painting as a messy business, and he would decline to wear a smock and a beret. On the way to Eve's studio, he stopped at the café for a dozen hot biscuits, then walked over to Unc Knobby's store for a quart of fresh honey sealed in a mason jar.

Unc Knobby, thin, stooped, his yellow skin spotted with age, bent Bodey's ear about the hideous art his grandnephew Altimus Plato had shown in his shop—pictures of pimps and prostitutes and people shooting up.

The proprietor of the small grocery ran a hand over his bald pate and shook his head. "I says to him, dis is a holy town. What you showin' dat trash fo', and he says to me white folk like to buy from po' boys who grew up in da projects. I says, 'Altimus, you grew up here on Main Street,' and he says back, 'Whatever sells, Unc Knobby.' Disgustin'. You want to take a pound of butter wit' dat honey?"

"Sure." Bodey managed to escape Rainbow Liquor and Food while his biscuits were still warm.

With his art supplies in their big Hobby Lobby bag along with the sales receipt on one arm and the box of biscuits and grocery sack of honey and butter on the other, Bodey arrived at Eve's place and elbowed himself into the studio. Eve looked up from her position on the floor where she executed stretches on an exercise mat. His heart beat a little harder as she arched over long legs clad in slim yoga pants and her cropped top rode up showing a bare midriff. She posed in front of a huge canvas showing an enormous live oak thrusting up from the soil. Between its branches, a landscape full of small figures faded away toward infinity.

"Right on time," she told him. "I've been up since dawn working on the commission. After a few hours, I get knotted up and take a break to stretch."

"Another thing we have in common. I used to do stretches before I rode. Saved me from a lot of pulls and sprains, I think. Didn't do diddly for broken bones though. You have breakfast? We can eat these while they're hot, then stretch out on the floor together if you want."

"I'm all finished stretching for the morning. I think I had a glass of orange juice around seven. Yummm, Rainbow Café biscuits and fresh honey. This isn't going to keep the over-thirty flab away." She took two. "There's coffee in the carafe on the counter by the sink."

Bodey filled a mug and watched Eve neatly break her biscuits and slather them with butter and honey using a clean, plastic palette knife. She bit in with her eyes closed and licked a dribble of honey off her chin as if she wanted to savor every lard-laden crumb. Ethereal, my ass, thought Bodey. He figured Eve had wells of untapped sensuality. As part owner in an oil enterprise, he knew where he wanted to drill.

He left his coffee and crossed the room to place his hands on the naked flesh between the cropped top and the drawstring pants. Bodey licked the crumbs off her lips and tasted the honey in her mouth. He ran his hands under a soft sports bra and felt her nipples harden. Though her hands came up, she didn't push him away. This was going so well, they could be doing it on that exercise mat in the next few minutes. He'd release her hair from that tight braid, part it with his fingers, and…"

"Eve, you in there? I need to take my lesson early today. I have an appointment with my hairdresser at ten." Renee Niles, or whatever she called herself now, pushed into the studio. Bodey didn't recall her hair being quite so red, or her eyes that strong bright green, or her boobs swelling that large, but she looked even better than old memories recollected.

"Sorry I interrupted," Renee said with a smile showing all her teeth between bronzed lips.

Eve burrowed into an oversized T-shirt splotched with paint. The back of her neck turned red. "No problem. Bodey is here to paint, too," Eve mumbled as her head emerged.

"I can see that. Remember me, Bodey?"

"You are unforgettable, Renee."

"I'd like to think so. Where can I set up, Eve?"

"Ah, over there. Bodey, do you have your canvas board? Set it over here."

"Yes, ma'am." I've also got a hard-on stiff as a board, Bodey thought as he rummaged in the Hobby Lobby bag and laid out his paints and brushes.

"Good. Did you bring a picture you want to paint? Let's clip it up here in the corner. Why don't you sketch it on your board while I check Renee's project."

Renee's project, Bodey could see, was an anatomical study of a well-built black man's back and buttocks. Lots of deep purple lines denoting hollows in the muscles dominated the dark brown study done on a real canvas, not this board thing he figured beginners used. She worked with oils like the Old Masters. That defined Renee—experienced at everything.

Eve suggested Renee pop out the purple with some cad yellow contrasts. Bodey watched almost embarrassed as the women ogled the black dude's picture, though Eve's interest appeared solely professional. He scratched his pencil across the canvas board in an attempt to draw a bucking bull with the rider on its back using perfect form. He used one of his championship photos and hoped Eve would notice.

"Okay, Bodey. Put a good-sized dab of each color on your palette arranged like this color wheel and a big gob of white. Now try to rough in the background. If you go over your sketch a little, it doesn't matter. Acrylics dry fast. You can paint it in again. I'm going to work on my painting while you do that. Holler if you need help."

"Aren't you going to show me how to hold the brush?"

"Whatever works for you, Bodey."

"Yeah, I've heard that before," he mumbled and began slapping paint.

"My therapist said I should take up my old hobby to help me get over men. Think it's working? I don't," said Renee squinting at her subject's firm ass.

"You paint pretty good, Renee."

"If Eve is busy, you can call me for pointers any time. I expected to hear from you before now."

Bodey didn't answer. He continued to slop away until Eve returned. "Hmmm, don't try for so much detail yet. Just try to capture the energy of that bull," said Eve bending close.

"Eve, I've finished mine. Check it over for me." Renee drew Eve back to her side of the room. "I don't know what to paint next—unless Bodey would pose for me."

"Clothes on or off, darlin'?" Bodey said automatically. "Eve owes me a portrait."

"From the waist up only!" Eve protested as Bodey started to strip off his shirt. "Leave the shirt on."

"Whatever you want, honey." Bodey took a seat on a stool.

"Wait, do you have a hat. You need a hat."

"Got my lucky hat in the truck."

Bodey retrieved it. The hat was black and battered and had a dented silver concha band around the crown. "Always won when I wore this hat," he reminisced. "Damn good hat."

"I think I remember that hat," Eve said.

"Like I said, my lucky hat. I always wore it when I had something hard to do."

"That old, holey T-shirt isn't working for me, Eve. Please, can't he take it off?" Renee whined.

"Fine. Take off the shirt, Bodey, if it doesn't bother you."

Well aware that he was trim and hard-muscled, Bodey took off the T-shirt so slowly his act would have done credit to a Bourbon Street stripper. He tossed it in a corner like a rag and slouched on the stool. He turned his pretty side toward Eve, but she motioned for him to turn the other way where a long, pink scar slashed through his tan across the ribs and around his back. A bull named Yellow Thunder had gored him during the dismount after he rode out the clock. Stitched up and bandaged tight, he'd completed the competition, come in first, too. He told the women that story as they worked. It wasn't bragging because it was God's own truth. About the time Bodey's back started to bother him, Eve said they had to clean up so she could make her class at the Academy.

Bodey shrugged into his T-shirt and casually strolled around to take a look at the canvases. Renee had nearly completed her version. Bodey barely recognized himself. He knew he was well-muscled through the shoulders and chest, but she'd drawn a cowboy on steroids with bulging biceps and six-pack abs. Renee had taken the artistic liberty of portraying his jeans as unzipped nearly down to his crotch—as if he were some Abercrombie and Fitch model. All his scars had vanished. Bodey guessed she flattered him. He'd had more than his fair share of women and had no problem strutting around naked in front of them, but to show him like that in paint somehow made this cowboy uncomfortable.

Bodey moved on to view Eve's canvas. She had scrubbed in his figure but given most of her time to the face. His stance, his scars, his eyes, though very blue, seemed to say here sat a man sore and weary, looking for a light in the window and a warm bed where he could rest. Did Eve see him like that?—a worn-out man with no one waiting at home. Who would want to marry a man like that? Who would even have sex with this guy?

Renee came up beside him. "Well, Eve doesn't do portraits very often. I think mine is better. Help me get my things to the car, will you, Bodey?"

Bodey picked up her picture of the buttocks gingerly by the edge and hefted her rather heavy wooden box of art supplies while Renee carried her still very wet cowboy canvas carefully out to a black Lexus.

"Maybe we could do a private session at your place or mine to finish this up," Renee invited with her hand on Bodey's arm.

This close, he could tell the green eyes came from colored contacts. The darker roots of her hair showed around the crown of her head, hence that trip to the hairdresser she'd mentioned. As she pressed against him, her breasts felt harder than he remembered. Was there anything real left of Renee Niles?

Eve watched the old friends and lovers standing so close together. What a fool she had been doing that stretching routine for Bodey Landrum's benefit. Leave it to her to come up with such a feeble attempt at being seductive. For a short while, she'd begun to believe he was very attracted to her. The kiss at the fireworks, the arm he had kept around her waist, the lip-locking this morning that might have led to sex, all of it was probably engraved in Bodey's genes like the startling blue of his eyes. She carried her own art gear to the trunk of her old, white Toyota, placed it inside and gave the lid a slam that made both Renee and Bodey jump apart. Eve got into her car and turned the ignition. She'd be early for her class, but didn't care.

"Hey! My stuff is still inside," Bodey called as she pulled out.

"I'll keep it safe for you. I'm late. See you next Tuesday."

"I haven't paid you!" Bodey waved two twenties at her.

She stopped and rolled down the window long enough to take one of the bills. "Since this wasn't a private lesson after all."

"Renee took the other bill from Bodey's fingers and handed it to Eve. "My share. I'll pay you back next week, cowboy, or maybe before. That's eight on Tuesdays, right Eve?"

Eve shrugged as if it didn't matter one way or the other to her. Then, she peeled out spraying bits of broken oyster shells from the driveway on her students.

Chapter Four

Renee Niles Bouchard Hayes finished Googling Bodey Landrum on her home computer. He began to take shape in her mind as more than a passing amusement, perhaps husband number three. From her comfortable home atop one of the small hills in her daddy's subdivision, she could just see the roof of the Three B's mansion, a house twice the size of the one she lived in at the moment.

Marriage, Renee felt, should be a well thought out business decision, not some silly Romeo and Juliet affair like her stupid cousin's involvement with Noreen Courville. Everyone knew the Courvilles didn't mix with the Niles family because of some ancient grudge and pushing Noreen and Rusty together in that barn had been a hoot.

As Noreen, a student of history and lover of genealogy, told Renee—ad nauseam—the previous attempt to end that feud through marriage had been around 1843 when the youngest son of Maxime and Marguerite Courville went on a sudden two year grand tour of Europe. The eldest daughter of Aaron and Ramona Niles had broken off her engagement to Rufe Courville and married a local doctor while the young man travelled and so caused more bitterness between the clans.

None of Noreen's family, except for her brother,

the priest, had come to her and Rusty's tiny and rushed wedding in the nun's chapel at the Academy. If Renee hadn't volunteered to be maid of honor and taken charge, the whole affair would have been a shabby disaster. True, the feud died down upon the arrival of the first grandchild, but Renee didn't feel family grudges faded that easily. She knew she'd never forgive her own weak-willed mother.

Bodey would want children, probably. Renee guessed she could endure one or two if he insisted. After all, women these days had epidurals and tummy tucks and nannies. Hardly anyone died giving birth. She'd had the same thought about her carefully chosen first husband, Elias Bouchard, a noted and wealthy heart surgeon, who thought he had picked Renee as his trophy wife after ditching the sagging Liz, mother of his five children. Fortunately, Elias had no desire to ruin another woman's body with childbearing.

But in the end, she had grown bored with her husband's long hospital hours and devotion to golf and deep-sea fishing. How had Liz endured the man for so many years without indulging in an affair? Renee had taken four lovers over the span of her marriage—her tennis instructor, her personal trainer, the yard boy, and the pool man. When that afternoon storm blew up, she should have realized Elias would come home early from a day at the links and find her straddled across her trainer on a weight bench, but she had been too preoccupied with the man's marvelous stamina to hear the thunder, the same thunder masking the arrival of her husband's car. She despised Louisiana weather.

Fortunately, Elias was an intellectual man and not given to violence. Rather soft, the doctor could never have taken on her hard-bodied trainer anyhow. He satisfied himself with stripping his roving wife legally of everything but the furnished house her daddy had given them as a wedding gift and a few pieces of nice jewelry. If she hadn't delayed having children, she would have gotten a much better settlement. Make a mental note—when she married Bodey start a family immediately and get it over with.

Renee reviewed the Landrum assets again, a few million dollars made on the rodeo circuit invested in oil and a Texas ranch, a line of western clothing, endorsements for saddles and blue jeans and who knew what else, and of course, the newly inherited Three B's Ranch and its contents. His body was great, his face handsome, his temper easy-going unless riled, and he'd had staying power in the sack when they'd gone together in high school—but he wouldn't be indulgent like her second husband, Gerald Hayes.

Renee had found Gerry, bless his weak ticker, a long, bad year after her divorce. He'd been faithful to his fat, diabetic wife until death did they part but was ripe for a well-deserved, shapely, good-looking reward forty years younger than himself. Gerry did everything to please her. He paid for the boob job even though he said her real breasts were a treat, but she needed to renew her confidence after being dumped by Elias. Gerald took Viagra against his doctor's orders to please her in bed and died on top of her. Even the nitro she'd forced between his lips hadn't revived old Gerry nor her rather out of practice attempt at CPR, a skill her first husband insisted she learn. His children got everything except for the Lexus, some lavish personal gifts, and a modest cash bequest that kept her comfortable for the past year. Now, she need to husband hunt again like a vampire badly in need of blood.

Bodey Landrum possessed money, looks, and a crude charm. Renee thought she wouldn't be tempted to stray for a good long time during which she would make the sacrifice and have a baby or two. At least, Bodey had no other children to suck up his fortune. He wasn't likely to die on her either. On the other hand, if he ever did catch her cheating, Bodey seemed like a man who might take physical revenge on her lover. She'd noticed some scars on his knuckles, maybe from bull riding but possibly from brawling. Strangely, that held some appeal for Renee who shivered deliciously at the thought of men fighting over her.

Who else was there? Not Red Courville who enjoyed playing around on his attractive wife, but would never leave her or their four kids. She'd given him a brief try and had no intention of being only a well-kept mistress. He'd use up her remaining good years, then find someone younger. Nope, her next husband had to be Bodey Landrum.

****

Bodey Landrum looked hard at himself in the mirror. Okay, he had a few tiny lines in the corners of his eyes from being out in the sun too much. He had a lot of scars, but none were disfiguring. Some women liked them. He kept trim now by doing ranch work rather than going to the gym, though during his career he had worked out. His tan was real, not man-made. His dark hair grew thick on top and without any gray. True, he kept it clipped short or else his curls grew out long and girly. Some women preferred men's hair to be long enough to be gathered in a horse tail like that Evan Adams. Maybe Eve was one of them.

He stood several inches less than six feet tall and was squarely built. Sure, the gals liked longer, leaner men—men with gaunt cheeks and dark eyes like pet cocker spaniels and beaky noses like golden eagles. He regarded his own blunt nose, bright blue eyes, and the cleft chin with a hint of dark beard. Mama always said she thought his daddy might have had Irish blood.

Too bad Bets hadn't asked, or maybe remembered, his father's name at that party where she'd had too much to drink and gotten pregnant by a total stranger. The man had passed through town with the rodeo, and Bets did love a bull rider. He'd had beautiful blue eyes was all she could recall. Often, she'd laughed and said Bodey must look like his daddy because he sure didn't look like her. Betsy Landrum never saw Bodey's sire again, though she'd taken Bodey to the rodeo every year since birth and tried to match up faces. It was a hard thing to know about your mother.

Bets had put off telling him for sixteen years. Even being in the midst of hormone-driven teenage lust himself when his mama finally came clean hadn't helped much. To know that his own mother once had been, well, like Renee Niles, or the women he'd slept with on the circuit, was hard to take, but that hadn't stopped him from accepting their offerings.

After all these years, Renee would have given him a tumble if he'd gone home with her this morning like she wanted. She was still a good-time girl, and they'd had some fine sex between his birthday and the end of his senior year when he'd hit the road to do some rodeo before college started. He had the experience now to know Renee had been a fairly sexually accomplished seventeen-year-old. They'd hooked up now and again when she attended college, once at Noreen's wedding in fact, and she'd been even more skilled then. With two husbands behind her, she probably had the experience of most high-priced call girls by now. His mother would have been proud that her son hadn't been very tempted.

He was rich and ready to settle down. He stood up straight and looked at himself in the mirror again. Bodey Landrum was prime property. So, why wasn't Eve showing more interest? Both times when he kissed her, he'd felt her on the verge of cracking open like a big dungeon door suddenly letting in the white, hot light of day. Both times, the door slammed shut. It galled him that maybe the key to that door lay in the hands of a horse-maned, eagle-beaked, puppy-eyed artist named Evan Adams ready to turn.

****

Eve took her lunch at the Academy as usual. She sat with the two elderly nuns who had influenced her the most during her school years. At the time, she thought of them as ancient, when in reality they had been in their late fifties and vigorous. Now, Sr. Helen's arthritis and a palsy prevented her from teaching the art classes, though she still taught French. Sr. Inez, a candidate for hip and knee replacement, rarely went riding anymore. The shortage of nuns and a desire to help a former student led to Eve's taking over their specialties.

Eve swallowed a spoonful of Lenten bean soup. A roll of crusty brown bread laid broken open but untouched at the side of her bowl. She picked at the small, green salad and drank some of her iced tea. Sr. Inez and Sr. Helen exchanged glances.

"You're very quiet today, Eve. Are any of the students giving you trouble?" Sr. Helen asked slowly and gently, her white curls bobbing along with her head under the short veil she still preferred to wear.

"I can come lay down the law for you," Sr. Inez, whom the girls called Nessy behind her back and whose friends used the nickname to her face, offered with relish. She'd been a martinet in her day, but her students always learned their lessons. Those she favored, like Noreen Courville, went on to win prizes at the Social Science Fair. She still taught history, having given up her post as riding mistress with reluctance.

"It's not that. Two men I used to know have come back into my life recently, and I'm not sure how to handle them."

"Men," said Sr. Helen. "We aren't the best people to ask about men."

"But, we are willing to listen," Sr. Inez offered.

"Thanks. I'm not sure you can help. You see, I—ah—lived with one of them for a year while I attended art school." Eve blushed.

"We are well aware such situations exist," Sr. Inez said. "Go on."

"Around the time my mother got sick and moved to Houston, he moved to the west coast. I was supposed to follow him after graduation, but I couldn't leave my mother."

"But he wrote, called, kept in touch, and loves you still?" Sr. Helen asked as she raised a spoonful of quivering cherry Jell-O to her lips. The doctor said gelatin might be good for her old bones and couldn't really be considered a sweet even during Lent.

"Well, no. Our communications stopped after a few months. By the time my mother died, I had no idea where he lived. Now, he reappears in Lafayette doing some sort of installation for Red Courville."

"Did you try to find him all those years ago?"

"No. I needed some time alone, to work on my art, to gather my energy."

"And that time has turned into ten years. I remember when you returned here worn out and in debt." Sr. Helen nodded emphatically to show it wasn't just her old age palsy.

"This place heals."

"We hoped you might join our order," Sr. Inez remarked.

"I considered it, but something held me back. I can't define it."

"Tell us about the other man," Sr. Inez urged Eve.

"I hardly know him really. We spoke only once when I attended here. I thought he might be interested in me, but he started dating one of the other girls at the Academy, and he never gave me another glance. Oh, I had a silly crush on him. Those blue eyes, a rodeo rider, kind of dangerous, he had everything going to attract an immature schoolgirl. Now he's back in town and, well, taking notice of me. Or so I thought until his old girlfriend showed up."

"Bodey Landrum and that—" Sr. Inez clamped her mouth shut tight.

"Renee Niles. We remember. Every time Fr. Cyrus heard confession from that girl, he looked as if he'd aged a year. We feared Bodey might come to tempt you after he stopped you on the bridle trail. Sr. Nessy told me all about his lurking under the oaks that day and how you arrived late back at the barn," Sr.Helen revealed. "Oh yes, I recall him well waiting for the Niles girl after classes, a very handsome young man with blue, blue eyes." She gave a wispy sigh.

"He's probably sown his wild oats by now, and a man who is good with horses might be a good man," Sr. Inez said thoughtfully.

"Perhaps the artist became involved with his work but never forgot you," Sr. Helen weighed in.

"I feel awkward with both of them. I'm just not good at dealing with men."

Sr. Helen considered. "Men like blondes, I believe, and you are a blonde. Maybe if you wore your hair loose, it would help."

"And wore more fitted clothes," Sr.Inez said looking at the baggy, paint-speckled shirt that hung to Eve's knees. "Not that we're advocating pre-marital sex, but you can't catch fish without bait."

"That's what Ja'nae Plato suggested when she loaned me one of her dresses. It might have worked, but then Hardy Courville and Renee Hayes got all mixed up in it, and I just don't know if I want to try…"

"Life again?" Sr. Inez suggested.

"Perhaps you should take your problem to the Holy Mother. The Blessed Virgin had a husband and a son. She'd know about men," Sr. Helen speculated.

"I'd suggest Mary Magdalene. She had more experience," Sr. Inez said.

"I suppose prayer is always worth a try," Eve answered. She collected the trays, stacked the dishes for the two nuns, and carried the dirty dinnerware to the kitchen.

"Eve will need some temporal help as well if that Niles ho—" Sr. Inez started to say.

Sr. Helen put a finger to her lips. "Don't earn yourself an act of contrition, Nessy. Your knees and hips are too bad. I do think we need to check out these two men and give Eve our advice and some assistance. She deserves some happiness, but only with the right man."

"My thoughts alone about Renee will earn me a penance. I have an idea."

Sr. Inez gave Eve a beatific smile on her return. "Eve, dear, would you consider giving two old nuns a ride to the Lafayette Art Walk next week? We do want to see your landscape in situ as well as your friend's sculpture."

"Of course. I'd be happy to take you." Eve suppressed any regrets she might have about being saddled with two elderly nuns who could barely walk. After all, these two once strong teachers had given all the years of their lives praying to God and guiding young women like her. It was the least she could for them. She put aside any thought of inviting Bodey to go with her.

Chapter Five

The week turned long on him again. Bodey Landrum got the floor people started early on Monday ripping up the gold shag carpet and preparing the surface of the slab to take a nice wood veneer. He'd found some good antiques among the stored furnishings, but the orange velvet upholstered couch and chairs he'd donate to Goodwill. The living room needed leather that dogs could drool on and kids could kick without doing much damage to the furniture.

He'd tried every day since Tuesday to get Eve out of her studio to ride or to eat dinner or to take in a movie. She worked Wednesday through Saturday nights at the restaurant and put in all the time she could on the commission from Hardy Courville because the piece needed to be done for the grand opening. Valid excuses, but underneath he sensed her uncertainty either about him or Evan Adams just like he could when he mounted a young bull for the first time. He began to feel uncertain himself, not a good emotion for a man who always brimmed with confidence.

Renee Hayes called him almost as often as he called Eve. Finally, he'd treated his former girlfriend to an expensive lunch in Lafayette for old times' sake, but when he claimed he had to meet his interior designer right afterward, she'd followed him home and dogged their steps, making suggestions about the house. Renee was still hanging around when the frustrated decorator left. Bodey knew Renee could show him a good time, but Big Ben had taught him to set a goal and go after it without dilly-dallying along the way. Not his idea of a wife and mother, so why waste his time on her? He'd sent Renee home by saying he had to go for a haircut, the male equivalent of "shampooing my hair."

Bodey went out to the machine shed and passed a few hours with Rusty working on a hay baler they'd want to use later in the spring. When his cell phone rang, he nudged it open with his chin to keep the oil off the surface.

"Hi, Renee. Sure, you can use the pool, but the water is still fairly chilly. No, I'm up to my armpits in grease right now, will be for most of the day. People are tearing up my flooring all over the house, so I'm stayin' out of the place. Thanks for the offer, but I think my shower still works. Some other time, then."

Rusty raised his eyebrows. "Looks like Cousin Renee is on the prowl again."

"We're old friends, that's all. Like I said, I'm lookin' to settle down."

"Sure you are. What did you do Saturday night while Eve served fried crawfish tails at the café? Us old married men need to live vicariously."

"So I went to the Rainbow Express out on Highway 90. Doesn't mean anything."

"You went to a honky-tonk, and it didn't mean anything."

"I had a few drinks. I danced with these girls who were celebratin' a birthday until my knee started to bother me. I came home, took two Advil, and went to bed around one."

"How many phone numbers did you get?"

"Three, not my best night, but I don't plan on callin' any of them since I found out Eve is still available."

"I keep trying to tell you this is not a good match, old friend. The two of you couldn't be more different. She's all artsy and stuff, and you're all cowboy."

"Not true. We both like horses and strawberries and Mama Tyne's biscuits. I buy art. She makes it. We're both pretty much alone in the world. You and Noreen had less going for you than that." Bodey wiped his hands on a rag.

"We're both from old families around here."

"Old families who hated each other. Noreen was Miss Rich Academy Girl, and you were just another cowboy whose daddy lost his land. Her people didn't even come to your wedding, just me, your dad, a few of her college friends, and the nuns."

Rusty carefully put down the wrench as if tempted to use it on Bodey. "You can be as generous as Big Ben and just about as dense when it comes to personal relationships. We get along with her family fine since Jesse came into the world. Noreen is a partner with her sister running the bed and breakfast in the old Courville plantation house. Hardy drops by when he has a project out this way."

Bodey knew for a fact Noreen worked with her sister to bring in extra money since she'd never gone back to college to do her student teaching after Jesse was born, but he passed over that since Russ turned all red and thin-lipped when he mentioned their shotgun wedding.

"Hardy Courville is Noreen's brother? Sure, I

remember now. He looks more like a bigger, heavier, richer version of you. Noreen is so short and has all those dark curls. They don't look much alike."

"Now I know you aren't from around here. Hardy is one of the red Courvilles."

"I know that's what he calls himself, but his hair isn't all that red."

"Noreen claims the youngest Courville son way back when was fathered by Aaron Niles, one of my great-great-great grandpappies. Now and then, a Courville still pops out looking like a Niles. Noreen proved we have the same male ancestor in a paper she did once. Hardy makes jokes about it."

"So you and Noreen are really related? Not good."

"By now, no more than most families who have lived in the area a long time, less than a lot of the Cajuns. Early on there was almost a case of incest, but the Platos say old Mother Leontine, who founded the school, intervened with an early warning and some sage advice overheard by a slave woman working at the Academy. Ja'Nae and Leon are that woman's descendants. Noreen interviewed them about their family stories. She wants to write a book someday about the Niles-Courville feud. Remember, Noreen used to say she thought we were the reincarnated souls of those lovers being given a second chance. Noreen toned it down when Jesse got old enough to understand. She didn't want to upset his Catholic upbringing for now, but I'll bet she tells our daughter later. Women, you never know what they'll come up with."

Bodey shook his head to clear it of the romantic slop he'd had to listen to the whole time he and Russ went to college. "See, that's another thing I have in common with Eve. We aren't from here. Her daddy came from up north somewheres, Wisconsin or another cold place, and her mama grew up in Mississippi. I checked what I could of her family tree. Lots of information on the female side. Those folks are family proud. Dead Confederates sprinkled around everywhere."

"An absolutely great combination, Bodey, the offspring of a southern belle and a Yankee meets a Texan who looks like an Irishman and doesn't know who his daddy is. Didn't you used to call her Miss Fancy Pants because Eve thought she was too good for you?" Still smarting from Bodey's earlier remark, Rusty looked like he wished he could suck those words back into his mouth again.

He had a wife who loved him, children, and a sense of family that went way back, the only things Bodey didn't have. In their younger years, they would have been beating on each other by now. Bodey seemed determined to take the insult well.

"The great American melting pot, that's what it's all about, bro. We've done all we can with this machine. Call in a repairman if you can't get it going. Give the bill to me since we'll be sharin' the hay. I think I'll clean up, get some lunch, then take Rocky out for a good hard ride. He's getting soft on spring grass and oats."

Rusty nodded in agreement to all of the above. "Aren't you afraid Renee will be swimming in your pool, her nipples poked out about an inch from that cold, cold water?"

"Your cousin is a temptation, not a phobia, Russ. I figure I can flirt all I want, but if I'm gonna live here I need to keep it zipped. Rocky isn't the only one who needs a good hard ride."

"Enjoy the rest of your day, then, Bodey."

"I plan to."

****

Eve knelt in the pine straw in front of the statue of the Magdalene. Her offering, a splotched red and white camellia blossom lay at St. Mary's feet. Eve's eyes were on the same level with a small plaque that said a Courville had donated the image in memory of his mother, a strange choice of gifts she'd always thought. The statue of the Virgin and Child sitting inside a circle of flowers directly in front of the main school building at the Academy had a similar plaque with a dedication from the Niles family. Although she tried to keep her mind on her prayers, Eve couldn't help but notice that the Sisters had placed the Magdalene at the farthest reaches of the Academy's grounds in a grove of tall pines. They encouraged women with something to repent to walk a wandering and contemplative path to get here, out of sight of the pure souls being taught at Mt. Carmel.

Eve had walked here three times recently, this last in her riding boots which had worn a blister on her heel, but she thought this small pain might be part of the price to pay for an answer to her jumbled prayers. Should she give in to Evan who had been calling often and consider moving to the west coast with him? Ethan hadn't mentioned marriage, just artistic opportunities.

As for Bodey Landrum, the daydream of her teenage years, she'd thought he'd call her after their encounter on the bridle trail so long ago. She imagined she'd play hard to get. They would flirt and go riding together. Eve never got farther than that because the next day Renee Niles boasted to her clique about how good Bodey performed in the sack, or rather the rice hulls. After that, it was Bodey and Renee, Renee and Bodey, until he had gone away to college. No woman in her right mind would wait all these years for a daydream to come true.

Lately, she had been getting strange vibes from Hardy Courville as well. Probably, she only imagined that he stood too close and gave out compliments too lavishly. Then, he'd ordered the commission the day after the art walk and wanted it in three weeks, promising her $10,000 if she had the masterpiece ready in time for the opening. Seeing her with her hair unbound, wearing a very little black dress, and having two men fawn over her, appeared to have opened Hardy's eyes to more than her art. She possessed not a drop of confusion on how she felt about Hardy. He was a married man known to have bad intentions. The word lecher described him.

Entering a convent retained a certain appeal, especially now. Despoiled by Evan and art, she'd parted from that path years ago. Still, becoming a nun wasn't beyond the realm of impossible. The Catholic Church had a shortage of nuns, and as Bodey said, she'd lived chastely here in Rainbow. A life of quiet contemplation, some time to paint, some time to share all she knew with her students, both spiritually and artistically, no men to confuse and upset her, would be rewarding.

Then, why hadn't she moved in that direction before now? She heard Sr. Helen telling her all over again that taking holy orders must not to be used to escape life. Eve knocked her head gently against the rocky base holding the statue of the Magdalene, who with her unbound, long hair, bare feet, and flowing garments barely covering her breasts certainly looked as if she had all the answers when it came to men. No answers came to Eve.

****

Bodey galloped along the Academy's bridle trail making Rocky sweat a little. New grass colored up spring green. The golden oak pollen in the air and the vision of Eve bouncing ahead of him on her little dappled mare drew him on, but when he nearly reached the old brick stables belonging to the Academy, he slowed Rocky to a walk and prepared to turn around. Off to the left he saw a path he didn't recall. Perhaps, the trail was new since he'd last lived here or had been hidden by bushes just leafing out again after winter. He knew retreat cottages that hadn't been built yet when he was a teen sat scattered in the piney woods behind the school. Rocky veered that way, and Bodey let him have his head.

The path was narrow, hemmed in by thickets of young longleaf pine saplings and made more for walkers than riders. Bodey could barely hear the sound of Rocky's hooves on a trail cushioned by years of fallen pine needles. He came around a bend into a wide clearing circled by red azaleas in bloom. There in the middle of the glade stood a statue to some Catholic saint and a woman pressing her forehead against the marble base. Wilted floral offerings left by others lay scattered over the pine duff. The long blonde braid, the little black bow, her riding clothes, told him the woman was Eve.

He'd interrupted a sacred moment, and his

conscience said he should leave as quietly as he had come, but the devilish part of him residing mostly below the waist started sending fantasies to his brain. He was a marauder who had come across a virgin praying in the woods. She was meant for the convent, but after he swept the woman onto his horse and ravished her in a secret glade, they could not be parted—because he was so great in bed, and she really did not want to be a nun. Yeah, that sounded about right.

Rocky moved forward. Bodey couldn't remember having given the horse the signal to do so. Eve looked up. He held out his hand. She took it, and bracing herself against the base of the statue, he pulled her onto his saddle. Bodey turned his horse toward another path he knew beyond the pine grove. They followed a coulee that once drained the Courville's sugar-producing land. As they came up on the narrowest part of the ditch, Bodey urged his paint horse into a gallop and gave him an extra kick that carried them all across the trickle of water in the bottom.

Eve laughed and pressed against him. She dreamed of course. Exhausted by her confusion and prayers, she'd fallen asleep. A gallant cavalry officer had come riding along to whisk her away from the dangers of war. He would take her to a secluded, safe hideaway and make passionate love to her, swearing to return after the battle to ask for her hand in marriage. She'd had this dream before. The man always possessed Bodey Landrum's blue eyes, cleft chin, and fetching scar.

The coulee widened as it approached the point where the stream entered Bayou Boueux. Trees completely engulfed by wild wisteria in full bloom covered the little delta. Lavender drapes of blossom smelling of honey fell from the tips of the water oaks to their roots. Animals had broken a pathway into the center of the tangle. Bodey dropped Rocky's reins to the ground, slid off his horse, and lifted Eve from the saddle. Stooping, he led her through the opening and out into the clearing.

Don't talk and ruin this fantasy, Bodey thought, but Eve, being a woman, had to say something. "It's like a cathedral in here."

Okay, a cathedral, kind of disturbingly religious for him, but he did intend to worship her. Signs of the animals who had broken the pathway abounded—a few beer cans, a brown liquor bottle, and a used condom Bodey stepped on and hastily kicked aside so the pale purple petals covered it. Horny teen animals, he figured. Renee brought him here once, but they'd been scared off before things went too far by the sound of boys hunting squirrels in the vicinity. Renee claimed Noreen used to hide out here when she was a kid to get away from her family, but clearly, only big kids used the area now. Vaguely, he recalled Rusty and Noreen going to their "secret place" all the time. Could be the spot, and what was good enough for Rusty was good enough for him.

Bodey took Eve to the center of the hidden glade. He kept his eyes open as he kissed her, checking for snakes and thanking heaven March was too early for the mosquitoes to be really bad. Then, he did what he had always wanted to do, flick that little black bow onto the ground and loosen Eve's fair hair with his fingers, kissing her all the while. She opened her mouth for him and closed her eyes.

Without sight to distract her senses, Eve felt the heat of his body penetrating her clothing. The hum of the bees in the blossoms grew louder, the smell of the honey sweeter. The pressure of his fingers opening her plain white blouse moved down her center, then around her back to unhook her simple cotton bra. How disappointed he must be with her clothing flitted through her mind, but she refused to open her eyes to see. No dream, this was no dream at all, but reality at its finest.

Bodey flung the blouse and the bra aside, seeing only the whiteness of her skin, the pink tips of aroused nipples. He took one in his mouth and suckled. Eve's knees slowly buckled. He sank to the ground with her.

The riding pants presented no problem, held up as they were with a zipper and a single button, but those high, black boots were going to be hell to get off. He could take her just like this, but he wanted Eve naked, completely naked, and sprawled on the bed of lavender petals. She pulled his shirttails out and ran her hands up his back and down into his jeans where the fit got so tight there wasn't much room to spare. He laid her down, centered himself over one leg, and tugged the boot off, then repeated the process on the other leg. He stripped off the jodhpurs and cotton panties without even noticing them.

Eve lay with her eyes still shut and a small smile on her lips, her pale hair wild about her. Bodey felt grateful for the closed eyes because now he had the awkward task of getting out of his own clothes. Oh, he knew cowboys could get away with making love with their boots on, hats too, for that matter, but he wanted to go to extra effort for Eve. He parked his backside on the ground, heaved off his boots, and got out of his jeans. His blood heavy penis springing free was almost painful. Bodey searched the jeans still smelling of cigarette smoke and spilled beer from Saturday night, grateful he hadn't gotten around to doing the laundry when he found the two condoms he'd shoved in a back pocket out of habit.

Eve waited, determined to live in just this moment of bees and blossoms and Bodey Landrum. She heard the thump of boots, the crackle of plastic, and her mother's sharp voice in the back of her mind. "Men get what they want, and then they stray. It's their nature. Do you think that artist is going to remember you out in California where all the women are whores? After I die, become a nun and pray for your father's rotten soul, Eve."

"Bodey?" she said softly to drown out the inner voice. "Bodey?"

He answered her by running the tip of his finger along her cleft, stroking the soft hair between her legs. He went deeper, found the spot, and rubbed lightly until her breathing became panting. Then, he mounted and rose over her. What a wonderful ride!

Eve could feel nothing but Bodey along the length of her body from her fingertips to the pads of her toes. Deep inside her pelvis she tightened, tighter and tighter, until there she experienced an explosion like the fireworks on Art Walk night. "God, Bodey!"

Hearing his name right alongside of the Almighty gave Bodey the incentive to go for two. His bad back or bum knee might give out, but for now, he was feeling no pain, quite the opposite. "Open your eyes, Eve."

She managed to raise her lids briefly but then they fluttered shut again, her pale lashes against her flushed skin. Her gray eyes did turn smoky when she came. Eve writhed and bucked under him now, almost throwing him off, but Bodey Landrum, four time All-Around Cowboy, intended to ride down to the last second. His own release was all the better for it. As his pace slowed, Eve pulled Bodey's head down for a series of lavish kisses, she still high on sex, he fading. He rested finally between her snowy white breasts.

The bees interrupted by turmoil in the glade returned to work. A mockingbird nesting in the tangled vines sang a crazy warning song. "Guess we should go soon," Bodey said yawning. His bad knee was beginning to stiffen, but the old back had held up.

"I don't ever want to leave this place, Bodey."

"I know the feelin', honey, but someone is sure to send a search party if we don't go back. Here, let me brush you off." He shook lavender petals from her hair and swept crushed blossoms off her back from her shoulders to that beautifully formed behind that had attracted him as a horny teenager. Maybe, he wasn't finished after all. Bodey nibbled Eve's neck.

"I could eat two boxes of strawberries," Eve said, crouching to pull up her pants.

"I'm clean out, but we could stop by the store and get some."

"No. Hardy Courville is coming by to give me final approval on the painting. He wants it hung by Friday afternoon."

"Cancel with him. We can get some whipped cream, too."

Bodey kept kissing her neck as she tried to snap

her bra and put on her blouse. He remained stark naked. "I can't afford to offend the art patron. It's a big commission. Help me with my boots," she pleaded.

"Yes, princess." Shooting her a disappointed glance, Bodey took a second to put on his jeans. Eve pointed her toes and leaned on his shoulders as he knelt and drew the boot up to her knee, first one, then the other.

"Need help with yours, Bodey?"

"No, ma'am. A cowboy who can't put on his own boots ain't worth shit."

"Are you sulking?"

"After you, princess." Bodey found his lucky hat and swept a bow over it as he had done once before. As Eve left, he picked up the discarded condom, wrapped it in fallen leaves, and packed it out of the glade leaving it undefiled by them. Damn Hardy Courville and all the Courvilles before him.

Chapter Six

A good night's rest eluded Bodey Landrum. When he slept, he dreamed of Eve, sometimes with himself, sometimes with Hardy or Evan. When he woke, he wanted her right beside him. Finally at six a.m., he got up and drove halfway to Lafayette to a truck stop that carried fresh Krispy Kreme donuts. He bought a dozen assorted and headed for Eve's studio. If he got there by seven, they would have a whole hour together before Renee showed up for the painting class.

****

Hardy Courville stood back from his commission painting and then moved closer gradually. Eve gave him a miffed look because he hadn't kept his appointment late yesterday afternoon. Though he had apologized and explained about a major client showing up just before closing and expecting to be wined, dined, and treated to a "date" with one of girls at the gentleman's club he frequented, Eve suspected Hardy had treated himself to some sexual pleasure as well and left her waiting for his arrival. Now, he gave Eve all the stroking he could muster. The check for ten thousand jutted from his shirt pocket. He plastered on the words "pleased" and "delighted" referring to her work.

Up at seven a.m. and dressed in leggings and a long-sleeved, light blue tunic with a neckline scooped low enough to show a little breast, Eve had not expected the man to show so early. She quickly pulled on a man's shirt so old it had worn thin in spots and closed the middle two buttons over her chest when she saw him at the door. But her hair, Eve hadn't taken time to braid it this morning. She wished she had. He stared at her as if spinning fantasies about her loose tresses, how her locks would wrap around his fists and slide along his belly if she went down on him.

Crowding against her, Hardy moved in close to the painting.Through the branches of the live oak, he could make out the Courville Plantation, the Academy, rolling hills, lowlands and ponds, wading birds and patches of Louisiana iris, a small sunning alligator among the many details. He claimed the landscape reminded him a little of those Chinese wall hangings where hundreds of tiny creatures went about their daily lives. "Perfect, Eve, it is perfect."

He slung a heavy arm across her shoulder, and its weight popped the two closed buttons open. Hardy had a good view down her front now, and that couldn't be accidental. He'd never come on to her before that art walk a couple of weeks ago. Maybe, the sloe-eyed, somber saints she painted—or the fact she taught at the Academy and hung out with nuns—warded him off in the past. Darn Ja'nae Plato for loaning her that skimpy black dress and the great Bodey Landrum for drooling all over her like a Top Ten bull. Hardy Courville was a man who loved to compete for a contract or a woman someone else wanted. Eve felt fairly sure he'd felt her up to determine if she wore any underwear that evening and probably bragged to his cronies about her being braless. And what if Evan Adam told tales about their times together at art school when she'd been young, naïve, and willing to try most anything with him.

"Eve, you live in the moment like no other woman I've ever met," Adam used to tell her as they lay naked on his futon. "Come to San Francisco with me, be with me."

He hadn't mentioned marriage beforehand though, and her mother became too ill to do without her only child. If Evan did the kiss and tell with Hardy, the contractor would only go after her harder. She knew his type. He'd glory in defeating both an artist and a bull rider for her attentions, but he was her art patron and she must handle him carefully. Now, Hardy let his hand dangle down her chest.

Renee Hayes had babbled about giving Hardy the "marriage or nothing" speech not too long ago at one of her private lessons, so Hardy remained in the market for another mistress. He probably assumed that Eve as an artist was a Bohemian, sort of a hippie, and didn't have the word "marriage" in her vocabulary. All these years alone and supposedly living like a nun, she might have been practicing free love unbeknownst to him, and he'd just gotten a whiff of it when Bodey and Evan came on the scene. Hardy Courville never missed an opportunity, any opportunity.

"Eve, baby, you are wasted out here in the country. I just finished up a nice row of townhouses in the city. You could live in the suite downstairs and have your studio upstairs close to that good northern light you artists are so fond of. Wouldn't cost you nothing. We could work out an arrangement. You could paint all day. No more teaching and waitressing. I'd come over evenings, join you for the lunch hour sometimes."

Eve went still under his arm. She wanted to shrug

Hardy off and tell him to go to hell, but the commission check hadn't changed hands yet. She could pay off a nice chunk of her mother's bills with that. It didn't say much for her morals that she stayed quiet. Yesterday's actions with Bodey didn't say much for her morals either. All night long, she'd wanted to call and tell him she was lonely and wanting him, but her mother's sour voice had come back to haunt her. "Chase men and they'll never chase you."

Finally, she'd gotten up and put the finishing touches on the commission. "I—" she managed to get out, but the sound of a big-engined truck coming up the drive cut off her reply.

Hardy waited for an answer as booted feet clomped across the stepping stones. The door began to open. "Think about it, baby, your own place free and clear, and nothing to do but paint and take care of ole Red." He took the commission check from his shirt pocket and transferred it to hers, giving her breast a squeeze along the way. "See you Friday."

Bodey Landrum stood framed in the doorway. His expression said, Unhappy To See You, but he didn't say the actual words.

"Bodey, my man, great to see you again!" Red Courville strode over to the door and shook hands. "Looks like you brought breakfast for two starving people. Give me one of them chocolate donuts with sprinkles. Eve told me earlier you were taking lessons from her. This one yours? I can see the bull in that slash of gray, and the cowboy hanging on for dear life in the blue and brown diagonals. This is my kind of abstract, lots of energy. Frankly, I don't get Evan's stuff, all those vertical lines and little dots."

"It's my first one," Bodey said numbly. He cocked his head and still saw only a really bad painting.

"I'd give you five hundred for it, but you might get a better offer at the art walk in the city. Eve, you be sure Bodey shows this picture in my lobby along with your things."

A car with an engine that purred, thanks to the generosity of Gerald Hayes, came up the drive and slid easily into a space between the two oversized trucks. The sound of high heels ticked across the paving stones. Renee Hayes burst through the doorway.

"Am I too early? I couldn't wait to continue my painting!"

Bodey checked his watch. Seven-fifteen. He held out the donut box in Renee's direction. She plucked out a plain glazed, ate it in four sharp bites, then licked each fingertip as she gazed at Bodey.

"Thanks," she said, as husky-voiced as if they had just gotten out of bed together. "This is exactly what I needed to start my day."

"Well then, everyone is very early for class this morning. Do you want to paint or pose first?" Eve asked, twisting the tails of her shirt between her hands.

Bodey plopped the box beside the coffeemaker without offering Eve a selection. He peeled off his shirt, hung it on the side of Renee's easel, took a lemon-filled donut in one hand and an apple crumb in the other, and assumed his pose on the stool. "I'm totally at your service, ladies," he announced, giving Renee a cheesy smile.

"Mind if I stay a while and watch the creative process?" Hardy pulled a chair next to Eve as if to claim his turf. He hunkered down there with another chocolate donut and one topped with coconut and a cup of coffee.

"Eve, I think my front view of Bodey is finished. I'll scoot my easel around and do him from the back this morning."

Bodey paused with the last bite of the apple crumb donut half way to his mouth. "So long as you keep my pants on, Renee. If you plan on displayin' this at the art walk, I don't want my rear hangin' out for all to see. Got a scar back there I ain't too proud of."

"I haven't seen your rear in a good long time Bodey Landrum, but I recall it as prime," Renee said. "Besides, I have no place to show my paintings unless Hardy offers me space." She shot an enticing smile at the contractor.

"By all means, use my new lobby, Renee. You and Eve and Bodey are all welcome. Evan will have some paintings on display, too. I like to patronize the arts all I can. Courville Construction will have the best exhibit in town."

Bodey sank his teeth into the second donut, and lemon filling squirted out on to his naked chest. He scooped the blob on to a finger and sucked the jelly into his mouth, his eyes on Eve. Already deep into painting, she didn't appear to notice, but Renee sucked in a breath. Hardy Courville stretched out his legs as if he meant to stay a while.

After half an hour, Bodey called for a break. He stretched his ripped body, hands over head. He was no six-footer like Courville over there hoovering up another donut like a vacuum cleaner and slurping more coffee, but he didn't have a rich man's gut on him either.

"Mornin' coffee has about passed through me. Could you point me to the facilities, Eve?"

"Second door on the right," she answered without taking her eyes from her work.

Bodey exited into the little courtyard and entered Eve's home. The bathroom was a small box of a place with one little window where Eve had hung a panel of stained glass in a wisteria pattern for privacy. A big, claw-footed tub, looking heavy enough to sink through the old floorboards, occupied most of the space. Large enough to hold two, he figured. Held up on an old-fashioned ring and pole clamped to the tub's edge, a blue shower curtain with a pattern of silvery fish shielded it. A half-dozen fat pillar candles of various sizes and shades of purple, blue, and green sat on the tank top of the plain white porcelain commode. The mirrored medicine cabinet had been set into a frame of old cypress boards.

Bodey took care of business, then flicked open the cabinet while he washed his hands with the speckled ball of handmade soap taken from its place in a large scallop shell. No sign of a man showed in its contents. It held a little pink ladies' razor, some sort of feminine deodorant, the usual aspirins and bandages anyone would stock. He flicked aside the shower curtain, saw a light ring around the tub, but no dark hairs or red ones either. No beard hairs in the sink, and Courville was freshly shaved. He went back to posing, relaxed and sure Courville hadn't spent the night. Even better, Hardy had left in his absence.

Bodey posed another half hour, then said he wanted to paint. He set the painting of the bull aside and got out another canvas board from the supplies he had abandoned at the studio the previous week. Eve frowned.

"Don't you want to work on your rodeo picture some more, Bodey?"

"Hell no, not if Courville will pay five-hundred for it as is. Why mess with perfection? I have a new idea." He started smearing in a background of lavender, white, and deep purple, consulting Eve on how to get a flesh tone.

"White, yellow ochre, and a touch of crimson. You can lighten or darken it depending on the age and sex of the person."

At the end of an hour, anyone clearly observing knew that Bodey Landrum was painting a nude. The figure emerged, naked and pale, from his background. Her long blonde hair covered what were obviously breasts and both hands folded primly over her pubic area. Renee, bored now that Bodey no longer modeled, wandered over and asked rather acidly, "Who would that be?"

"I call her Eve—the one from the Bible, of course."

"Well, if you ever want a real model, you just call me, Bodey Landrum."

"If I ever paint you, darlin', I'll call the picture *Hellfire and Damnation* or maybe *A Wild Red Rose*."

Pleased, Renee went back to her work. Eve continued to concentrate on her own painting, but her cheeks turned red. At nine-thirty, she declared the session at an end since they had started so early. As Bodey and Renee cleaned their brushes, Eve stretched from side to side glancing out the window at another lovely spring day. A black SUV, the sort of vehicle a soccer mom might drive, turned into her lane.

"Probably another bored housewife in search of a hobby," Eve speculated.

Evan Adams parked and climbed out of the SUV. He took a rattan picnic basket from the passenger seat and carried it over Eve's stepping stones, his soft loafers making no noise at all. He noticed Eve at the window, gave a cavalier sort of wave in her direction, and entered the studio without knocking. He kissed Eve on the cheek, no air between lips and flesh this time, Bodey noticed.

"Eve, dearest, I brought breakfast. Croissants from that marvelous French bakery on Pinhook Road, imported ham shaved so thinly you can see through it, a selection of cheeses, and—fresh strawberries, your favorite. If I've caught you between classes, perhaps we could dine alfresco on your charming patio."

"I'm starving. How did you know, Evan?" Eve joined her students at the sink to wash her hands.

Bodey counted the donuts in the box. Six left. So jealous of Courville, he hadn't offered her one, and she hadn't taken any for herself. All the time he kept an eye on Red, this snake in the grass was sneaking up on Eve with croissants and strawberries in a basket. Maybe the Bible had gotten the fruit of temptation all wrong.

"Where'd you get the ride, Adams?" Bodey sneered. "Borrow it from the convent?"

"My gracious and generous hostess, Amanda Courville, loaned me her vehicle for the morning."

"Does Hardy know you're out here bothering Eve when she needs to finish her commission for him?"

"I find Red Courville knows very little but has the money to make up for that deficiency."

While Eve cleaned up for the alfresco breakfast,

Evan strolled around the studio, peering at the works in progress and studying Eve's big canvas. "Nice work, Eve. Not my style, but nice. Looks finished to me."

He came to Bodey's nude. "Obviousy the Bibical Eve done with sort of a Rousseau-like primitivism, but much more crude. This is yours, Bodey?"

"Yeah, it is. I haven't painted the snake in yet. He'll be long and dark like the cottonmouths I shoot over in the coulee."

"Indeed." Evan raised his eyebrows.

"Trade you some donuts for a ham and cheese croissant. We could warm 'em up in the microwave. Paintin' does give a man an appetite. Renee, you stayin' for second breakfast?"

"I shouldn't after that donut. Well, just a nibble, a few strawberries."

The four of them crowded around Eve's tiny porch table, Bodey knocking elbows with the left-handed Evan more than necessary. He made sandwiches out of the elegant repast and jumped up to warm them in the microwave. Eve seemed more amused than angry. Evan was peeved, definitely peeved. Bodey managed to draw out the time it took to eat the simple meal until Eve had to leave for the Academy.

"Now wasn't this fun?" he said giving Evan's hand a hearty shake.

"Delightful," Evan answered, his face pinched like he was getting a shot in the rear.

"How come you always talk like some kind of continental dandy, Ev?"

"Evan's father is in the diplomatic corps. He's lived all over the world, Bodey," Eve answered for her former lover. "How are your parents, Evan?"

"Dad passed away two years ago, heart attack. Mum remembers you well and would like to see you again if I can persuade you to come to San Francisco with me. Have you finished thinking about it?"

"A move like that requires much more thought than I've had time to give it," Eve said evasively. "We'll talk after the art walk. So sorry about your father."

Let's see, Bodey calculated. The married Hardy Courville wanted Eve as his mistress if he hadn't mistaken what he observed upon arrival, or she could go to San Francisco with Evan and lead a glamorous life that probably did not include marriage or children either. He'd planned to do more courting, but now it seemed he needed to get a lick in sooner, put his own offer on the table before the art walk. That gave him five days to convince Eve to marry him. He could do it. Bodey walked with Evan to the SUV and gave the sculptor a friendly slap on the back. "I'll be at the art walk, too, Evan, old man. I'll be there with Eve."

****

Eve picked out the tiny, pink shrimp dotting her salad and took a sip of hot tea. She broke up a quarter of hard-boiled egg with her fork and mashed it into the greens.

"Not hungry?" Sr. Helen inquired. "The salad looks delicious. Wish I could have coffee, but with my tremors, well, I am grateful for the iced tea. We must be thankful for what God gives us even though it might not be exactly what we think we need."

"I had a late breakfast with Bodey Landrum, Evan Adams, and Renee Hayes." Eve concentrated on demolishing another quarter of egg.

"More interesting than eating with two old nuns,"

Sr. Inez commented.

"More awkward certainly—two men who have known me in the Biblical sense, and Renee who is trying to turn an old flame into a full-fledged forest fire."

The two nuns exchanged glances while Eve kept her eyes on her food and felt her face redden.

"We're not your confessors, Eve, but we take it that there has been a change in your relationship with Bodey Landrum."

"I went to pray in the pine grove. Along came Bodey riding one of those paint horses he favors. He held out a hand, and I went with him—just like that."

"It wasn't a—rape?" Sr. Helen said in a whisper she could barely force past her vocal chords.

"Oh, no, entirely consensual. That's how weak my character is."

"A blue-eyed man on a paint horse would be hard to resist, not that you shouldn't have tried," Sr. Inez added. "Perhaps, it was meant to happen. Surely, Bodey will…"

"Do the right thing? Make an honest woman of me? Sisters, that went out in the Sixties."

"Doing the right thing never goes out of style," Sr. Helen said with an emphatic head bob.

"At least, I know I can resist Hardy Courville's offer to—take care of me."

"Hardy is married to one of our girls, Amanda Dwyer. She was a friend of his eldest sister and graduated about ten years before you. Amanda is lovely and gracious and very active in social causes, a perfect wife and mother. Whatever…"

"Would he want with me? Sex, of course, with

someone new and different. I'm sorry. I shouldn't have said that."

"We are so looking forward to the art walk on Saturday." Sr. Helen abruptly changed the subject.

Naturally, they wanted to leave the subject of extramarital sex behind. Eve gratefully dropped the topic as well. They were, as they had said, not her confessors.

"It will be my pleasure to take you. I need to get set up for the next class."

As Eve collected their trays and turned away, both nuns crossed themselves and murmured a brief blessing in her direction.

"Nessy, the Art Walk is only five days away and will require a great deal of prayer and divine inspiration."

"No need to tell me, Sister, no need at all."

Chapter Seven

Bodey put his plans into action by eating late Wednesday night at the Rainbow Café and sitting at the bar until Eve got off work. The trouble being for the middle of a work week, the bar stayed awfully crowded. Hardy Courville nursed a bourbon, and Evan Adams sipped a good merlot right beside him. At the far end of the counter, a trucker drank coffee. Bodey wondered if he waited for Eve, too, since everyone else surely was. The men acknowledged each other, but didn't talk.

"Last call, gentlemen. We be closing in fifteen minutes," the black, tattooed bartender informed them.

The trucker slapped down two dollars, got up and left. Hardy threw back the remains of his drink and stood up. Evan, unrushed, continued to enjoy his wine. Bodey left his last glass of beer half full. After five minutes, he beckoned to the bartender.

"When do you figure Eve will be done for the night?" He tipped the man with a five.

"Let me jus' check on that for you, sir." The young man inquired in the kitchen. "Miss Eve went out the back do' five minutes ago. She be home by now."

The three men walked out on to the porch together. "Headin' back to Lafayette...Red, Evan?" Bodey asked.

"Might as well. Looks like Eve doesn't want

company tonight." Hardy got into his truck and called to Evan. "Better get my wife's car home soon. She has some kind of committee meeting first thing in the morning. Going back to the ranch, Bodey?"

"Yep. After y'all."

He followed the other men toward the highway, and once they were on the limited access road, he did a U-turn on the other side of the underpass and drove back into Rainbow. The lights burned in Eve's house. She answered the door in her bare feet, a small glass of white wine in her hand. Her hair hung loose and finger-combed. Behind her, candles flickered in the tall blue holders he had purchased for her at the Rainbow Art Walk. The scent of honey filled the air, and that aroma took him right back to the wisteria-cloaked glade. Bodey didn't want to pressure Eve, but he was feeling some himself below the belt.

"I was waitin' for you. So were the others."

"I'm not in the mood to be someone's trophy tonight. My feet hurt, and I need to unwind."

"I know something we could do that would get you off your feet."

"Bodey—not in the mood. Can't you understand that?"

"Not what I had in mind. Come outside. The bugs ain't bad, and the night is beautiful."

Reluctantly, she stepped into a pair of slides and came out. Bodey led her to his truck where he took a thick blanket from behind the seat and spread it out in the truck bed. He lifted Eve over the tailgate. "Lie down. Here, rest up against my shoulder and look at the stars. There's Orion with his sword pointing right at Taurus, the bull. He'll soon be gone below the horizon.

Last chance for Orion."

"He's one of my favorites, too. I miss him when he's not in the night sky. My dad used to point that constellation out to me when we went night sailing. He named his boat after me, the Princess Eve."

"I recall that. Tough losing your father so young."

"Something you don't know—I broke up my parents' marriage. I wanted to see that boat so badly after he said he'd painted my name on the bow. I was around ten at the time. Daddy always went away weekends to work on that boat. I nagged my mother to take me out to the marina. Finally, she gave in, even though she didn't like to sail, hated being on the water, said it ruined her skin. The Princess Eve was docked in a private slip way on the end. Even before we got there, we could hear the music and the laughter. He had women on the boat, three topless women slicked up with body oil and sunbathing on the deck. Daddy was below entertaining a fourth. After that, Mother said she couldn't pretend they had a marriage anymore. The end."

"Kids aren't to blame when a marriage fails, Eve. You know that." Bodey placed a few tender kisses on her forehead, down her cheeks. "Heck, I don't even know my real daddy's name. At least, you knew your father loved you."

"What does that old song say—two lost souls on the highway to hell?"

"I think that last word should be heaven," Bodey insisted. He turned on his side and kissed her deeply, doing the tongue play for all he was worth. He stroked the breast Red had touched as if he were trying to erase Courville's fingerprints.

Eve wanted to go with him all the way to that cocoon of pleasure they had experienced before, but she put an end to it when they paused for air.

"I can't, Bodey. I need to go in." She got out of the truck and paused long enough at the edge of the lattice to wish him a good night.

Good night, sure. He had a long, painful ride back to the ranch.

****

Thursday evening, Bodey didn't bother to wait at the bar. He sat in his truck out back and called to Eve when she exited from the kitchen. Rebuffed last night, his rivals hadn't shown up. Bodey Landrum got ready to make his move.

She came over to his window and looked up as she leaned against the door. "I don't think this is such a good idea, Bodey, your being here again tonight."

"Come sit with me. I just want to talk. If you feel uncomfortable, the kitchen staff is still in there cleanin' up. You can go back inside any time you want."

"Last night, you were a stargazer. What are you tonight—cowboy philosopher?" Eve quipped, but she walked around the truck and climbed up into the cab.

Bodey had the radio turned low, but tuned into a station that claimed to be playing music for late night lovers. Not a very romantic setting out here by the dumpster, but Eve didn't seem inclined to invite him home or go anywhere else with him. He took a deep breath.

"I know you think we're too different to get along, but just consider for a minute. We have lots in common. We love horses and strawberries—and art. Yes, we both love art. Hell, we even have the same favorite constellation. And if you weren't fakin' it, we're sexually compatible, real compatible."

Eve's eyes widened under the glare of the security light shining through the windshield. "Faking it! You thought I faked it?"

"No! That came out all wrong. Some women do, but just forget I said it. What's most important is both of us are alone in the world. We'd be great together as a couple."

"Before you go any further, try to remember we've only known each other about three weeks."

"That's not true. We've known each other since we were high school age."

"We spoke once years ago, and that didn't go so well. You never tried to reach me again."

"I'll admit I got sidetracked with Renee, but you were always there in the back of my mind, waiting for the when the time came to settle down, my pure white convent rose."

"Hardly that! You never gave me a thought until you came into the café on your birthday. Confess."

"But I recognized you right away. Look, my folks, Big Ben and Bets, knew each other a few hours, and they went off and got married. Worked out fine for them."

"So you're saying I remind you of your mother."

"No way! You're nothing alike. Dammit, woman, you are makin' this harder than it should be. The only thing you got in common with my mama is that I love you both."

Now he had gone too far, too fast, but a beautiful smile blossomed on Eve's face. He could see it clearly in the glare of that star-eating security light.

"Bodey, Bodey. What am I going to do with you?" Eve took his face in her hands and kissed him so hard he thought he'd cut his lip on a tooth.

"Well now, you could…"

"Don't ruin this by suggesting I be your sex slave or some other nonsense."

"Would you be my wife, Eve?" Bodey thought he could have hit her with a two by four and gotten the same stunned expression.

"I said no nonsense. Three weeks Bodey, we've known each other three weeks and had sex one time. You've led an exciting life and probably slept with a thousand women. How could you possibly want to marry a quiet, thirtyish woman like me? You'd be bored with me the first year—just like my father was with my mother."

"I wouldn't say I've slept with thousands, maybe more than a hundred—but a gentleman don't keep count. I was just stayin' in practice until I found the right one, and I knew who she was that first night I saw you in the restaurant."

"Bodey Landrum, rodeo star, and me. It's simply impossible!" Eve moved fast then, getting out of the truck, slamming the door, and taking off in her own car as if some serial rapist chased her tail.

As humiliating experiences went, this soared right up there with the time early in his career when a bull ripped his jeans clear through the bicycle pants he used to keep his goodies in place and left him standing bare butt naked in front of the crowd. The only difference was the bull had left him with his balls intact and only a gash on his buttocks. This hurt a lot more. What had he done then? Walked away with a swagger and got ready for the next event that would win him the prize.

The next event, as Bodey saw it, was the Lafayette Art Walk. He knew Eve would be in the city all day Saturday hanging the exhibit in the lobby of Courville Construction Company's new building. Hardy and that snake, Evan, would be lurking around for sure, but he didn't want to crowd Eve at this point. He'd let her completely alone Friday and wouldn't set eyes on her again until he showed up for the unveiling of *Progress*.

Chapter Eight

The doors to the Courville Construction Company lobby remained locked with the refreshments and the rest of the art stowed inside. This guaranteed the crowd would stay in the small plaza for the unveiling of *Progress*, currently covered with a tarp attached to one of Hardy's cranes. Talk about overkill, Bodey thought. They could have gotten a model in a bikini to whip off the covering at the right moment. Only Red would use a crane as tall as his new three story building to remove a tarp.

Bodey searched for Eve's face in the group of art lovers and people who owed Hardy Courville their attention. She must be inside with all the others things Red was setting aside until he'd done his speech. The proud patron of the arts stepped up to the microphone and mumbled, "Is it on?"

Red began his spiel. "Welcome, Art Walkers. Today, we not only open the doors to the new headquarters of Courville Construction, second and third floors available for rent, but also proudly add our contribution to the cityscape. When I saw the work of Evan Adams on a business trip to San Francisco, I knew I had to bring his talent to Louisiana and show one of his marvelous installments."

Standing to Hardy's left the artist winced, then smiled as his patron turned toward him. Except for the festive addition of a Celtic cross worthy of the Archbishop of Dublin, Evan had dressed for the occasion in his usual crow black. Bodey felt glad he had dressed down in a new pair of his trademark jeans, a white T-shirt worn under a tan western shirt, all tucked in and belted with one of his prize buckles, and a simple necklace made of elk bone beads. He was presenting a clear choice here for Eve—a real man or some effete, self-absorbed art snob. Having left his hat at home, Bodey did feel a little naked but glad he had worn his most comfortable boots because it looked like a long evening, especially if Hardy didn't stop shooting off his mouth fairly soon.

As the sun set, Red Courville made a grand gesture toward the sculpture and the crane operator, right on cue, tugged his big-knobbed levers and raised the tarp. Bodey scratched his head. *Progress* looked like an aluminum rocket ship, maybe a sleek, art deco sort of rocket ship, but still some kind of rocket. The audience clapped politely. Hardy pressed a button on the base. The spaceship began to move on its springy narrow mount, thrusting forward, sinking back, thrusting forward through a shining metal oval—not a rocket ship in Bodey's mind anymore, but a giant aluminum penis heading toward a climax. Some people giggled, but most of the onlookers seemed to be hypnotized by the motion of the projectile through the ring. Their eyes widened. Their mouths fell half open.

Bodey searched for Eve again. He'd implied to his rivals that they would be together, but she hadn't asked him to accompany her. However, this absurd moment needed to be shared with the woman he loved. He looked across the installation seeking her and found instead Archie and Roger in their white suits, expressions of glee on their faces. Roger made eye contact with Bodey and gave his little finger wave. Bodey started to sink back into the crowd, but thought better of it and stood his ground. He returned the gesture with a real wave. Roger's eyes brightened. Then, Bodey put his hand down and retreated into the mass of people.

"Watch where you're going, cowboy," Eve's voice said right behind him. "Let the Sisters through to have a look."

"Oh my!" exclaimed Sr. Helen, placing a trembling, liver-spotted hand over the plain gold cross she wore at her neck. Her other hand rested on a cane hand-painted with tiny birds and flowers in brilliant oranges, yellows, and greens.

Sr. Inez murmured, "Saints alive!" and leaned heavily on the blackthorn walking stick a former student brought her from Ireland. The wooden cross on its leather thong around her neck bounced up and down as she coughed to suppress her laughter.

"Yeah, I thought it looked like a big ole—rocket ship, too." Bodey suppressed the urge to jump in front of their view and spare the elderly nuns—and Eve—the sight.

"It is rather, well, phallic, I suppose," Eve said delicately.

"That's the word I was lookin' for, phallic, that's the exact word." Bodey grinned.

"Sisters, why don't we move inside before all the chairs are taken? Red paid for some lovely refreshments. You can sit and look at the paintings," Eve suggested.

Bodey went first, breaking a way through the mob heading en masse toward the food tables while Eve shuttled her guests to the lobby. The elderly nuns creaked slowly toward a curvaceous love seat upholstered in burgundy leather occupying the center of the room after Bodey politely evicted two lounging teenagers with purple hair and multiple piercings.

When the male half of the matching couple raised an objection, Bodey leaned forward and whispered, "Look, they got free wine over there. If they won't serve you, I'll bring you some. Go try your luck."

"Frigid, cowboy dude," the guy answered and slouched away with his girlfriend.

"How nice of those young people to give up their seats." Sr. Helen lowered herself onto the cushy leather.

"And they say today's youth have no manners," Sr. Inez agreed. "Eve, you haven't introduced us to your friend."

"Sr. Helen, Sr. Inez, this Bodey Landrum, four time All-Around Cowboy, five time World Champion Bull Rider, male model, fledgling painter, and who knows what else," Eve announced.

"Exactly. I've got all kinds of potential. Pleased to meet you." Bodey raised a hand to his forehead as if he wanted to tip his hat, then let it drop to his side again not sure if a person should shake with a nun.

"Eve, dear, would you get me a napkin? My poor old eyes are watering from the glare off that sculpture." Sr. Inez chuckled softly. As Eve moved off, she added, "Doesn't our Eve look exactly like a bride tonight in that white dress, Mr. Landrum?"

Bodey regarded Eve's gown, a far cry from the sexy little black dress of the last art walk. Tonight, she dressed in gauzy white from her high lace collar and long sleeves down to the toes of her low, white sandals. Her braid wrapped around her head like a crown secured with pearl-headed pins and a single white camellia. In Bodey's opinion, she looked more uptight and locked down than usual, but still beautiful and unattainable.

"You don't have to hit me with an anvil, Sister. I proposed the other night. She shot me down just like she did fifteen years ago when I asked her out."

"Time and prayer, my son," Sr. Helen recommended.

"Yeah, I guess that is supposed to heal all wounds. Must work for some people."

Eve returned with a paper napkin and stood by while Sr. Inez dabbed her eyes.

"How about if we go get you something to eat and drink," Bodey suggested to gain more time alone with Eve.

"That would be lovely." Sr. Helen gave the couple a saintly smile as they moved toward the refreshments. She turned to Sr. Inez. "Strong, clever, and usually confident, I'd say. He's been bruised a bit lately."

"Perhaps too confident, so a little bruising won't hurt him," Sr. Inez conjectured. "He's definitely more suitable for our Eve than some artist who ran off to San Francisco when she needed his love and support. Bodey doesn't seem like a man who would run."

"Evan might have matured in the intervening years. Keep that in mind, Nessy. As for Hardy Courville, he is out of the question."

A slim, fortyish blonde wearing a sophisticated powder blue suit with a pencil skirt approached the nuns' couch. A silk scarf patterned with Van Gogh irises lay tucked under her jacket collar, the ends floating down her chest. She bent over to greet the Sisters, taking one of their hands in each of her own.

"I'm so glad you could come, Sisters. Eve must have brought you. She is so thoughtful. Are you enjoying the art?"

"Amanda Dwyer, so good to see one our best students again."

"It's been Amanda Courville for more than twenty years now."

"Yes, we know. How are all your beautiful children?"

"The eldest is at Tulane. My youngest daughter will be transferring to the Academy next fall."

"We'll be so pleased to have her, another generation of Mt. Carmel girls. Amanda, dear, could you possibly bring the sculptor over to speak with us for a moment? We so admire his work and our old legs simply won't hold us up for very long," Sr. Helen asked. She could see Evan Adams standing in front of one of his pictures, expounding on it for an audience of three.

"Of course, only give me a moment."

Amanda Courville crossed the room on her dyed to match pumps, placed a light hand on Evan's arm, and gestured toward the nuns. Adams seemed annoyed to be interrupted, but allowed himself to be towed over to the sofa.

"Our sculptor, Evan Adams. Have a nice chat while I go greet some of our other guests."

"Sit down, Mr. Adams. Don't fidget!" Sr. Inez ordered.

Evan set his narrow ass into the small space they made for him. He hadn't been to Mass since high school, but his upbringing forbade being rude to nuns.

"You're one of Eve's old friends from art school, aren't you?" Sr. Helen queried.

"An intimate old friend." Evan smirked, as if a nun would have no idea to what he was inferring.

"You want her to return to San Francisco with you."

"She'll never amount to anything in the art world in this backwater. She should come with me and develop her talent. I'll introduce her around, encourage her to explore new horizons."

"Eve will make a beautiful bride," Sr. Helen claimed, her head bobbing gently in time with her heartbeat.

"She was such a lonely child. Eve will want a large family, I'm sure. Hasn't she said so?" Sr. Inez asked her fellow nun.

"Our Eve will probably want a dozen," Sr. Helen said.

"No, no. What I had in mind was a creative collaboration. No children, messy little rug rats that they are. I am married to my art, you see, as you are to—ah—God, you understand." Evan squirmed in his seat.

"Children are the epitome of creative collaboration, wouldn't you say, Sr. Inez?"

"The epitome, and with Eve being such a good Catholic—"

Evan shot to his feet. "It's been so nice chatting with you, but…"

"Oh, sit, sit," Sr. Helen yanked at his arm far

stronger than she appeared. "Let's talk about your sculpture. It's so dynamic. I understand Mr. Courville paid $250,000 for that piece and took you into his home while *Progress* was being installed. He and Amanda must be very fond of you."

"As I am of them. Truthfully, I could have gotten twice that amount on the coast, but the Courvilles appreciate my work. I've been looking for new venues outside the bay area."

"Amanda was one of our Academy girls, you know. Isn't she a beautiful and gracious hostess? Did she show you around and see you were well taken care of in every way during your stay?"

"Yes, yes, beautiful, gracious, showed me around a bit, let me use her car. Now in *Progress* I was trying to capture the elemental …"

"Mr. Adams, we shouldn't keep you any longer. If you see Mr. Courville, would you send him our way, please? We do want to thank him for sponsoring this wonderful exhibit." Sr. Helen dropped Evan's hand.

For a moment, he looked like a captive animal unsure if the cage door had truly been left open. Then, he backed slowly away from the nuns. "So nice meeting you." Evan fled.

Bodey and Eve returned from the refreshment table, successful after a long wait in line. They carried clear plastic plates laden with little spinach quiches, bacon-wrapped shrimp, tiny hot dogs in a picante sauce, a small cluster of red grapes and a few wedges of fresh pineapple. Sr. Inez speared a wiener on a toothpick and popped it in her mouth. She fanned her lips.

"Spicy. Bodey, Eve, perhaps a small glass of wine." Off the couple went again.

Hardy Courville hastened over. "Sorry I didn't get to you sooner, Sisters. Are you having a nice time?"

"Oh, we are. Mr. Adams was so informative, and he just went on and on about your beautiful wife, how she accommodated him in every way, how they had such a good time in her car. Wasn't that what he said, Nessy? You must be so proud of Amanda," Sr. Helen gushed.

"No, Sr. Helen, I'm not sure those were his words. He did say how fond he was of Amanda, how lovely she is, and how they went around a bit. I can tell Amanda is a little lonely now that the children are nearly grown. I am sure Mr. Adams was great company for her while you were at work and the children attended classes. He seems to be a talented man in so many ways."

Sr. Inez nodded toward Evan who regaled rather loudly a cluster of young women with tales of the San Francisco art world. Amanda Courville joined the group and laughed at one of his anecdotes with her head tilted back, her light blue eyes sparkling.

Sr. Helen observed the scene. "Your wife is still a fine looking woman, even after giving birth to your four lovely children."

Hardy stared at his wife as if he hadn't seen her in years. Amanda always kept herself thin and impeccably dressed. He watched as she put a hand on Evan's shoulder and begged him to stop making her laugh so hard. The nuns glanced at each other, then back at Hardy like gypsy mind readers discerning his every inner thought—when was the last time she'd laughed at his jokes that way? When had he last told her a joke?

"So if you have everything you need, Sisters, I

have to take care of some business." Red couldn't seem to take his eyes off of Amanda as Evan gave her a fond squeeze of the shoulders.

"I thought he was after Eve," Hardy muttered under his breath. "Right under my nose, in my own house, and I missed it."

"Artists are so fickle in their tastes, don't you think, Sr. Helen? First one style attracts them, then another," Sr. Inez went on as if her sharp ears hadn't heard a thing. "Hardy, dear boy, I see another of our old girls over there. Would you ask Renee to come visit with us?"

"Sure, sure."

On his way to reclaim his wife, Hardy spoke a few words to Renee Hayes who stood by her three paintings and fished for compliments. Renee raised her eyebrows but strolled in the direction of the nuns, working her hips under a tight, electric blue dress with a sway worthy of a streetwalker on very high heels.

"Sisters, have you taken a look at my paintings yet? Remember, I got my start in your art class, Sr. Helen."

"I remember you well, my child. We took a look on our way in, but somehow I don't think Mr. Landrum wears his pants that low. Who modeled for the torso?"

"Oh, my yard man. Doesn't he have a delicious physique?"

"Certainly statuesque. What do you think of Mr. Adams' sculpture?"

"I find it rather suggestive."

Sr. Helen choked on a bite of quiche. Sr. Inez pounded her back.

"But worth $250,000. He told us he can get twice

that on the coast. Mr. Adams must be very well off. Sadly, he and Eve aren't compatible on the child issue. He doesn't want any, and Eve would probably have a dozen if she could. I fear for their relationship. Now if Mr. Landrum is as—ah, masculine—as you've painted him, Renee, well, that's a man who wants a family, perhaps a big family, to raise on a huge ranch in west Texas where you can see for miles and no lights shine on the horizon to blot out the stars. I'm just speculating, of course," Sr. Helen said sweetly after catching her breath.

"Excuse me, Sisters. I see someone interested in my pictures. I might have a sale." Renee hurried off to where two men in white suits regarded the paintings of Bodey, his front and backside, and the black yard man with lascivious smiles on their faces.

"Here you go, Sisters. Two white wines and two red. Take your pick." Bodey held out the glasses of red and Eve the white. Sr. Inez seized the pinot noir and tossed it back. Sr. Helen sipped on the chardonnay genteelly.

"Thank you, we were so thirsty from talking. If you would help us up, we'll take a closer look at the art now. You young people go and enjoy the rest of your evening."

"Find me when you want to go home. Nothing ever sells at an art walk. I don't have to stay all night," Eve told the nuns as they hobbled away, leaning heavily on their canes.

"Thanks, Bodey, for being so kind to them. The Sisters mean the world to me."

"Not their fault they're old and helpless."

"I guess we'll all be that way some day. Roger and

Archie are certainly taking an interest in your portraits."

"Now that just gives me the willies. Can we hide out somewhere behind a potted palm or something?" Bodey led the way toward a cluster of tastefully arranged plants the size of small trees. They drank their wine and watched art connoisseurs pass by.

"Hardy gave you the best place. He put your giant landscape on the wall nearest the food table. Lots of people are taking a closer look after they stuff their faces," Bodey remarked.

"We had an awful time getting it up there. Red had to send a truck and two men to move it. Then, we needed two more of his workers to mount the thing to the wall."

"I would have been glad to help if you'd called me."

"I don't feel right about asking you for favors. Besides, Hardy paid for it."

"I'd like to think we're still on friendly terms, that I didn't offend you by proposing the other night." Bodey watched Hardy Courville sling his beefy arm around his wife and whirl the slim blonde from the group around Evan Adams. He appeared to want to show Amanda something back in the offices.

"I didn't find your proposal offensive, just not…"

"Good enough for you."

"That isn't what I was about to say."

The Goth couple standing on the other side of the shrubbery snickered. The pierced young man spoke around the impediment of his tongue stud. "You can see her pubes and titties and everything. She looks like that blonde babe who waltzed around here a while ago with those freakin' old nuns. Think those dried up penguins

124

know what she does in her spare time?"

"No way!" His sooty-eyed girlfriend exclaimed.

"Way! Nude modeling."

Bodey peered between the leaves and caught sight of a very explicit nude hung at the end of a long line of Evan Adams' abstracts. "What the hell!" He burst through the plant barrier. The pierced teenagers jumped back so fast their third glasses of wine sloshed on their black clothing making an even darker stain.

"Hey, man! It's art, not porno, and you said we could have the wine, so cool it."

"Get out of here before I yank out that nose ring. I mean now!" Bodey said through gritted teeth.

"It's a free country, dude," the purple-haired guy claimed, but he backed away and drew his companion with him. Moving slowly to show they weren't intimidated, the teens slouched toward the exit, snagging two nearly full glasses of abandoned wine from a tray of dirty dishes. They beat it out the door.

Eve made her way through the leafy barricade. "What on earth is wrong with you, Bodey?"

"Go get Evan. I'm gonna stand here in front of this picture till you do. The man paints ten crappy abstracts that look like the ghetto on a bad day, and the only decent thing he hung is indecent."

"Let me see."

"No.'

"Move aside, Bodey, and let me see."

Bodey moved, then took up a position directly behind Eve, screening the painting from others.

"Well," Eve sighed. "It's an excellent rendering, but he should have asked my permission before he showed it. Obviously, he didn't hang it until after I left.

Venus Rising from her Bath, he calls it. I suppose he meant that as a compliment to me."

Eve backed up a foot and tread on Bodey's toes. "For heaven's sake, Bodey, it's art, totally imaginary, and very well done. Get a grip."

"Lordy Eve, you're comin' out of that big, claw-footed tub with the blue curtain. Your nipples are standin' out like you're real chilly. He even got the color of your short hairs right. It's a good likeness, but there's not a towel in sight. When did that snake paint this?"

"You're the one to criticize. Didn't you paint a nude of me from memory just this week and call it *Eve*. And weren't you using art to boast to Evan that we'd been together?"

"Well, yeah, but mine is kind of fuzzy, and you can't make out the features. Besides, your privates are covered."

"Don't you tell me those little pink dots peeking out of that white-blonde hair aren't nipples, Bodey, because I won't believe you."

"They aren't like real nipples, all standy-outy."

Bodey realized he'd gotten a little loud when he turned his head and saw the two nuns, Renee Hayes, Archie, Roger, and half a room full of art walkers staring their way. As for Evan Adams, he came striding across the room toward them obviously ready to defend his masterpiece. Suddenly, he tripped, falling flat on his face. Bodey shook his head. He could have sworn Sr. Helen's brightly painted cane whipped out for a second just as Evan passed her.

Renee went to the sculptor's aid. Digging deep into her cleavage, she drew out a white hankie reeking with perfume and edged in lace and dabbed at a cut on Evan's chin made by the flying Celtic cross around his neck.

"Are you all right, sweetie? Will you be able to sculpt and paint again because I simply adore your work? It would kill me right here if anything happened to these hands." Renee switched her grip from his face to his wrists and began to massage them.

"I may have sprained my wrist. I don't know. The new flooring must be slippery. I might have to sue Hardy if I am unable to produce."

"Archie, love, go get Mr. Adams some ice in a napkin. Quickly!" Renee ordered.

Much as Bodey enjoyed watching Evan Adams take a tumble, he still had a bone to pick with the man. "Eve, you stand right there. No, closer to the wall. Right there in front of the picture. I got to talk to Adams." Bodey cut a direct line toward the fallen artist, who attempted to rise with the help of Renee and Roger.

"Adams, I want to settle this without knockin' your front teeth down your throat, so I'm gonna offer you a thousand dollars for that picture of—of Venus, providin' I can take it down right now and put it in my truck."

"Don't be absurd. It's the best work I've done in years. I want people to see it. It represents a change for me from the abstract to a new realism. Besides, I could get ten grand for it on the coast."

Evan mopped his chin with the lacy handkerchief. Archie returned with the ice dripping in a paper napkin. Renee clamped it to Adams' left wrist with her hand. Roger dusted off Evan's rear even though the sculptor had landed on his face. The caterer's assistant rushed over with one of the elegant burgundy leather side chairs and placed it beneath the artist's backside.

"Done," said Bodey. "But it's cash and carry. I'll write you a check."

"It's not for sale to someone like you. Do you think I want my art displayed in some isolated ranch house, only to be ogled by ignorant cowboys who won't understand the moment I have captured?"

Bodey jerked Evan out of his cushy seat by his black silk turtleneck. "I said we have a sale. We are going to march right over to that table and find a space where I can write you a check for ten times what that piece is worth. Then, I'll take it to my truck." He frog marched the artist toward the refreshments.

"Are we talking about Eve or the painting? She might sleep with you, but she'd never stay with such a bumpkin," Evan sneered. He'd made a big mistake.

Bodey released Evan and drew back his fist, then hesitated just a second when he saw the horror on the faces of the nuns and Eve who now stood with them and not in front of the painting where he'd left her. Greedy excitement crossed the faces of Renee, Archie, and Roger as they looked on.

"Shit," he said and lowered his arm.

Evan Adams sucker-punched Bodey in the gut. Despite his pallid complexion, the sculptor packed a greater wallop than the cowboy expected. Bodey tensed his stomach muscles, and the cheap shot bounced off, bruising but not taking his wind.

Bodey raised his arm again, this time swiping across the refreshment table to where a plate of deviled eggs, their yolks swirled into fancy rosettes, rested. He raised the platter and ground the contents into Adams' beaky nose.

"Looks like you got egg in your face."

Bodey offered Evan a wad of paper napkins, but the artist decided to take another swing. Bodey blocked the punch with a shoulder and knocked his opponent to the ground.

"Now, I'll just write that check in the space I've cleared while you go clean up."

Adams wriggled on the floor with much more feigned agony than the light blow warranted.

"You ever play basketball?" Bodey remarked laconically as he wrote the check. "You got the height and the actin' ability."

Heavy footsteps pounded across the room. Bodey spun in case more trouble was coming his way. Red Courville charged to the artist's rescue with his wife's iris scarf hanging around his neck and his belt still unbuckled. Amanda followed him, buttoning her suit jacket over her wrinkled skirt. One tail of her silk blouse hung out the side of her outfit.

Bodey held up his hands. "Didn't mean to ruin your party, Red. I only wanted to buy a paintin' and intended to pay lots more than it is worth."

"I'll sue!" ranted Adams from the floor. "If I'm injured, I'll sue."

"Hush up!" Hardy ordered. "Bodey, my man, you okay? I saw that traitor throw the first punch from across the room, and I'll say so in court. No one around here doubts the word of Hardy Courville."

"But dear, we were—" Amanda Courville began. "Never mind."

"Adams, I'll put you up in a hotel tonight.

Tomorrow, you pack up your things and go back where you belong. Here's your pay off. We're through." Hardy held out a check withdrawn from the pocket of his gray suit.

Bodey offered the sculptor an arm up, but Adams threw it off. "You know Evan, all that yellow egg on your face offsets all your dark tones kind of nice." He tucked his check for Eve's nude portrait into the man's tight turtleneck as he had no pockets on his shirt. No way did Bodey intend to shove it in the man's pants, not with Archie and Roger watching.

"Bodey, I'll give you seven hundred for your *Bull Rider*. I don't like the way Roger Ames is looking at it, but I know he won't go that high," Hardy said.

Archie immediately said to Roger, "We must have a souvenir of this evening. It has been so delicious. Buy the *Backside of Bodey* for me, Rog. Oh, please!"

Hearing their words, Bodey shuddered. He hadn't gotten a close look at Renee's second portrait of him from the rear what with running around with the nuns and surely did not approve of its title. Not to mention, he knew he'd never worn his jeans low enough to show his crack, not ever. The back had those same big muscles she'd painted on his front and also lacked any scars he knew he had there. Could be someone else named Bodey, at least that's what he planned to tell people.

"If Renee will take two hundred instead of three," Roger bargained.

"It's a sale," Renee said before Bodey could offer to buy it to protect his own honor. "I must go to Evan." She crossed the small space to the west coast artist and knelt beside him. "You won't go to any hotel tonight,

Evan, dear heart. You'll come home with me and let me treat your wounds." She removed the check from his turtleneck and deposited in her cleavage.

"She'll fuck his balls off," Roger said to Archie. "Oh, sorry, Sisters. I forgot you were standing right there."

"This evening has been a little more than we bargained for, Eve, dear. I think Sr. Inez and I will forgo the other galleries and ask you to take us back to the Academy." Sr. Helen fanned herself with a shaking hand.

"Of course, I will," Eve answered, but her eyes followed Bodey as he crossed to the nude by the potted plants and took the painting down. He looked her way and headed the same.

"Bodey, you really shouldn't remove the art until the evening is over," Eve instructed as if he didn't know the etiquette of such things.

"The deal was cash and carry. That's what I'm doing. I'm in an art buyin' mood tonight. I want that one you painted of me, too. Name your price."

"You can see it's posted at five hundred, but I owe you another picture anyhow."

"Fine, I'll pay seven-hundred because I like it so much. I really do."

Bodey took a closer look at Eve's work. He wasn't sitting on a stool posing in the studio in her completed version. He sat on a fence with the gray-brown landscape of west Texas in summer stretched out behind him. The dust in the cracks of his boots showed and the sheen of sweat on his bare chest. All his scars and all his weariness were exposed to view. This cowboy looked ready to wash up and go inside after a long day's work. Eve called it *Going Home.*

"I kind of made a mess of this night. Maybe I *should* go on home."

"Back to Texas?" Eve asked with a little catch in her voice.

"No, I plan on stickin' here. Evening, Sisters." Bodey tipped his imaginary hat to the nuns, waited a moment for Renee and Evan to clear the exit out to the parking lot. Then, he thanked his hostess and trailed them slowly into the spring dusk.

"You know, Nessy, we should have been Jesuits," Sr. Helen remarked.

"Absolutely, Sister, absolutely, though I doubt even a Jesuit for all their wiles could have accomplished what we did tonight."

Eve shot them a puzzled look, but neither of the Sisters explained their remarks. "I'll bring my car around for you," she assured the nuns. "Wait by the door."

The nuns watched their former student's white form move into the coming darkness. Leaning heavily on their canes, they wobbled toward the doorway.

Chapter Nine

After a sleepless night, Eve had gone to early Mass because she was up anyway. Afterwards, she attempted to settle in for a few hours of painting before going to the café to wait tables for the largely tip-free Sunday buffet. The Platos had been kind enough to give her Saturday off for the art walk, and she couldn't complain. Even thinking about the night before made her head ache, and now, her ears rang, too. No, that was the phone. Who would call on a Sunday morning when most people were at church or in bed?

"Hi, darlin'. It's Bodey. I got to tell you I won't be paintin' this week. I have business out of town. I tracked down some cows from the line of Bodacious, the meanest yellow fucker who ever lived. I need to go check 'em out and make an offer."

"Only you, Bodey, would be interested in mean cows. I'm surprised you still want to paint, considering last night."

"Hell, Red gave me seven hundred for my little squiggle. I might have a real future in art. Now, don't get upset. I know he was payin' for my name signed in the corner. Would have cost him nothing written on a scrap of paper."

"That's the art world for you, fickle. Still, it wasn't a bad night for me entirely. After I dropped the Sisters off—poor dears, they slept most of the way back to the

Academy, too much excitement—I went back to the exhibit. A woman from Dallas approached me about doing a landscape with the Treaty Oak in the center— before it was poisoned, of course. She wants scenes of Texas between the branches and a bigger canvas. She didn't even flinch when I told her how much Hardy paid for his painting. Hardy had one of his work crews build the stretchers and staple the canvas, too. Of course, Hardy expected extras for the price and didn't get them. I'll have to pay someone to make the next canvas for me."

"That's a Texan for you, big-hearted, free-spendin' people. As for Hardy, I'm hoping you won't take up his offer."

"What do you know about that?"

"Overheard last time I was at the studio. You won't be movin' into his townhouse, will you?"

"No, I won't. I was trying to find a way to tell him without losing the commission—which doesn't say much for me. It's strange, though. Hardy barely bothered with me before he saw us together at the Rainbow Art Walk. Suddenly, he was pressing me for my favors. You gave him some competition, I guess. Then, last night, he never mentioned the subject. I had to detach him from Amanda and find a place to tell him definitely no. He wasn't upset."

"Hmmm," Bodey said happily. "Might have been a case of who has the biggest dick in the pasture when he saw us together, or that little black dress you were wearin', but whatever, I'm glad I didn't have to flatten a rich patron of the arts for you."

"Speaking of flattening people, I did *not* appreciate what you did to Evan. Okay, maybe I did. He was being obnoxious, but then, so were you."

"Dicks again, but I thought I was protectin' your honor. Now, that's a lie, and I'm not given to lyin'. About drove me mad to think you let him paint you nekkid, that you might have been with him and Hardy, too, after we were together."

"That shows how little you know me. If you had taken a closer look at the painting you would have seen Evan did it from memory. That woman is considerably younger than I am. She has no tiny lines near her eyes. Her breasts are higher, her waist and hips smaller."

"I'm lookin' at her right now. She catches the first mornin' light across from my big, lonely bed. She looks mighty good to me. It was the tub threw me off. I've seen your tub."

"You've seen considerably more than my tub and evidently didn't notice the details. You know, Evan used my bathroom, too, just like you did. As for your lonely bed, I'm sure you could fill it with someone more youthful than me.

"Your details are fine. As for my bed, I could have put three honky-tonk angels in it a few nights before I proposed, but when you're lookin' for quality, you don't go for common stock."

"Are you comparing me to your mean cows?"

"Nope. Never. I wouldn't do that, not ever."

Whoo-ie, that was a close one. He needed to get off the phone. As it was, he'd need a hand job or a cold shower fairly soon between the picture of the young Eve on the wall and the voice of the real Eve, low and warm, and maybe even teasing on the phone.

"Anyhow, I'm headin' for Oklahoma this afternoon. You'll be here when I get back, right? No slippin' off to San Francisco?"

"Judging by who comforted Evan last night, I'd say that yacht has sailed with another passenger aboard."

"Will you miss me, honey?"

Eve laughed, hearty and loud. She hung up on him.

****

Eve did miss Bodey Landrum. It seemed as if Bodey had ridden into Rainbow bringing thunder and lightning with him that first night and had electrified the town. When he rode out again, he took that energy with him, and the hamlet of Rainbow returned to its serene and isolated self.

His posse vanished, too. Hardy left Eve strictly alone. Renee Hayes called to cancel her art lessons indefinitely. She planned to take a trip to the west coast with Evan who had asked her to say good-bye for him. The coward, Eve thought. No apologies for painting her without her permission or his remarks at the art walk would be forthcoming. The great Evan Adams would crawl out of town on his belly exactly like he did the last time in Houston.

Eve should have appreciated the return to quiet and calm. She had the time to paint and research the Texas project without men showing up at her studio and calling unexpectedly. An advance allowed her to pay for the stretching of another huge canvas. She found a picture of the oak before it was vandalized, made a list of scenes she wanted to include, the Alamo being a must, bluebonnets instead of iris, cattle rather than alligators, more than enough to keep her mind occupied. The two large pieces would give back five years of life striving to pay off medical bills. Why was she restless? Why wasn't she happy?

Sitting at lunch with the Sisters, Eve absently asked them if she could bring them a dessert. "It's Lent, dear," Sr. Helen reprimanded.

"Sorry," Eve apologized, finally noticing that Sr. Nessy dined on a large, dark roll of bread and ice water. "I thought you usually fasted on Fridays."

"We are doing an extra penance this week. At our age, we are allowed a clear soup in the evenings to prevent our dropping over dead, but Sr. Helen and I have forgone it."

Eve smiled sadly. What could two elderly nuns have to atone for—impure thoughts? No, that one would belong to Eve come her next confession.

"Pride," said Sr. Inez. "Even at our age, we have pride in accomplishments whose credit should be given to God."

"Pride," Sr. Helen agreed. "One of the deadly ones. It wouldn't be gossip if we told Eve what we heard this morning. It would be spreading the good news, right, Sr. Inez?"

"I should think so."

"Amanda and Hardy Courville are going to renew their wedding vows right here in our chapel the last week in May on their twentieth wedding anniversary with a gala reception to follow on the Academy lawns. Their sons and daughters will be attendants, and there will be wedding cake!" Sr. Helen informed Eve with a glance at the dry stub of the roll remaining on her plate. "Gluttony, that's another one."

"I'm sure God will forgive you, considering the wonderful news. Don't most people wait until their twenty-fifth to do that kind of thing?" Eve asked.

"Amanda and Hardy have rediscovered each other

and could not wait, thanks be to God," Sr. Helen replied.

"And to all his saints," added Sr. Inez. "How are things going with the stimulating Mr. Landrum? I mean, how is he progressing with his art?"

"Isn't curiosity a sin?" Eve chided.

"No, I don't think so. Nessy?"

"Definitely not. This is a polite inquiry into the progress of one of your students, Eve."

"He's gone," Eve told them.

The sisters exchanged upset glances. "Gone, both he and Mr. Adams?"

"How did you know Evan had left?"

"Renee Hayes stopped by to tell me that she had sold one of her paintings at the art walk. Mr. Evans said her style would certainly draw attention in San Francisco. She went with him to pursue a career as an artist," Sr. Helen informed Eve.

"She was boasting, and never a word of thanks to her teachers or to God who gave her whatever talent she has," Sr. Inez snapped.

"Pride," said Sr. Helen again. "It's never good to have too much pride."

"About Bodey—has he moved back to Texas?" Sr. Inez nudged the conversation back where it belonged.

"Oh, no. He's going to look at some mean cows out west for his bull raising business."

"Mean cows and bull raising, an interesting man, Bodey Landrum, if a little rough around the edges," Sr. Inez reflected.

"Yes, but in some ways his manners are better than Evan's. At least, he seems sincere and doesn't look down on people of other races or with less money."

"Bodey has a good soul," Sr. Helen said with conviction.

"Well, I'm not sure about that. I think it might be sort of spotted like those paint horses he likes to ride. I just don't know what to make of Bodey Landrum." Eve sighed.

The Sisters smiled. "It will come to you with time and prayer."

Chapter Ten

Bodey studied the cows milling in a corral made muddy from an early spring rain as the animals looked for a way back to freshly green pasturage. Each cow showed the slight hump of Brahma ancestry and the yellow hide of the offspring of Bodacious.

Bodey glanced down at the man in the wheelchair. At first, he had been had thrown by the fact Connelly's ranch manager was a paraplegic, but once the conversation turned to cattle and rodeo, he'd grown comfortable with Patrick O'Shea and forgotten about the chair. O'Shea knew the business and did his job well, regardless of any handicaps. Bodey could respect that.

"Connolly said you could take your pick of the heifers, he's that pleased to be doing business with Bodey Landrum, but the cows with calf aren't for sale. Year or so, you'll be the competition."

"I plan on keeping the breeding operation small scale. I'm giving some thought to branching out into training bull riders, professionals and dudes lookin' for a thrill."

"That won't step on our toes any. Point out the ones you want, and Clyde will cut 'em out for you."

Bodey eyeballed the circling herd. He noted some of the feistier heifers who kicked out when crowded. "Let's load up the one with the stripes on her flank and

140

that black-eyed beauty over there. How about the one that's nearly cream-colored for the third?"

O'Shea motioned to the rider who moved among the cows, his horse working with him to isolate the chosen animals and steer them toward a chute where another hand waited to work the gates that would move the heifers into Landrum's livestock trailer. Cows with calves by their sides pushed their young protectively behind them and bellowed at the passing rider. Some lowered their heads and pawed the earth, more like bulls than cows. These were tough old ladies who wouldn't hesitate to take on any predator trying to get at their babies. Clyde and his mount ignored them and continued to pursue the black-eyed heifer.

"Now that's a pretty sight, a good man on a good cuttin' horse."

"He ought to be good. That's Clyde Michener who made his mark on the circuit doing just that. He retired maybe ten years before you did. Most of us are retired rodeo here. You have time for a meal? It's about nearly dinner, and the rest of the boys will be in soon. They'd all like to meet the great Bodey Landrum."

"Be my pleasure."

His big biceps pumping, Patrick O'Shea led the way to the kitchen. The man's chest had grown broad from years of controlling the wheelchair. Below the waist, denim covered two shriveled legs stuck into cowboy boots. O'Shea went up a ramp and through a kitchen door someone on the other side had left ajar.

"Wash!" a loud-voiced woman shouted.

"Sarah Ann, Clyde's wife. She's the cook, mouthy but not mean." Obeying, Patrick pulled up to a low washroom sink and scrubbed his hands with Bodey following suit.

Patrick parked himself at one end of the table and motioned to Bodey to sit next to him. Sarah Ann continued to bark from the kitchen.

"Wipe those boots. Hang up that hat. No one eats with a hat on in my kitchen." She placed two big tureens of beef stew chunky with quartered potatoes and onions and golden coins of carrots on the table, then slotted biscuits still in the pan between the steaming containers. Sarah Ann, cradling a wooden bowl, moved around clacking the salad tongs. "Y'all want salad."

"No, ma'am," said a young cowboy.

"You misheard me, boy. Y'all want salad. Eat your greens. Dressing is on the table. Pass it around. Sugar your own tea. Once I set down, I'm not getting up again." Sarah Ann made sure each and every side bowl was filled with salad before she took her seat at the other end of the table next to her husband.

Settling her ample hips, Sarah Ann announced, "Peach cobbler for dessert. Prayer before eatin'. This ain't the public schools." She swatted a hand that reached for a biscuit, but kept the prayer mercifully short.

"In case you haven't noticed, Sarah Ann is Clyde's wife but everyone's mother," Patrick O'Shea said to Bodey.

"She reminds me of my own, especially the hand-washing and eat your greens parts. Bets didn't cook much though. I took most of my meals at the diner where she worked. After she married Big Ben Barnum, she had someone to cook for her."

"Big Ben was a great guy. He never turned away a

cowboy who needed a meal or a small loan to keep going," Clyde Michener recalled.

"He put me on a calf at the age of eight, and I just kept going up in size from there. When I went on the road, he'd come bail me out of any trouble I got into and ream me out good for worrying my mother before he left. She's gone now."

"Yep, I remember when you were going for your fourth World Bull Riding Championship. You stayed on for an extra eight seconds in her memory. I was just a kid, but that was something to see," the young hand said.

He wasn't much more than a kid now, maybe nineteen at the most, but Bodey still felt a twinge of old creeping up on him. He switched the subject. "Clyde, I know you took a few buckles in your day."

"Mostly for roping and cutting, some steer wrestling. Me and Sarah Ann married young. She wouldn't have me doing any of the rough stuff when we had three boys to raise."

"Smart woman, Sarah Ann," Patrick remarked. "If I'd had a wife like her, I'd still be whole. Two ton bull came down on my spine when I was only twenty-one, one of Connolly's bulls. Wasn't Connolly's fault, but he asked me if I could use a computer. Of course, I couldn't. So, after I did my rehab and got used to my chair, he sent me off to learn. Said he was too damn old for that stuff and wanted a man who could keep track of bloodlines and the finances and bookings on a computer. He took the training costs out of my paycheck over the years because he said he didn't take on charity cases. He left me my self-respect. There's another good man for you."

Words of agreement passed around the table like the pans of biscuits. Bodey took a second biscuit and used it to wipe up Sarah Ann's rich gravy. The portion covering his plate was large enough not to be an insult to the cook. She smiled down the table at him.

"Your real daddy must have been proud of you, too, Bodey," Sarah Ann said.

"Never knew him. My mama said she'd introduce us if he ever passed our way, but that never happened. Big Ben taught me all I know." He never had told the press the circumstances of his birth and wasn't about to tell these strangers.

"We used to kid Pat when we watched you on the TV. He's got your eyes, I'd say, and that same chin. The resemblance is even plainer right here in person," Sarah Ann insisted.

"Any man would be proud to have Bodey Landrum for a son. He wouldn't hang back on bragging about it," Pat O'Shea said, shaking his head in denial and smiling at Bodey.

His smile, his chin, his thick, curly hair turned an iron gray, but most of all his blue, blue eyes, the eyes his mama could never forget, looked right at Bodey Landrum like a reflection that had aged him twenty years. Even as a prickly teen who didn't want mothering, Bodey had tolerated Bets running her hand over his dark hair and saying, "Your daddy had the most beautiful eyes, Irish eyes," when she'd had a few too many margaritas. Those eyes were his only clue to his origins. The biscuit he'd just eaten wadded up in his stomach.

"You ever do the rodeo in Lafayette, Louisiana, Pat? That's right down the road from where I'm livin'

144

now."

"I had the time of my life in Lafayette, big win, big party afterward. I swear I was still hung over a week later when I rode a bull for the last time. Maybe if I hadn't partied so hard my reflexes would have been better and I wouldn't be in this chair now. Hindsight. Hell, what does anyone know when they're twenty-one and think they'll never die?"

"I had my own worst moment around that age," Bodey said. Eyes turned toward him. Ears waited for a story.

"I was twenty-three, had just lost my traveling companion and best friend to a shotgun wedding. Ole Rusty, he always took care of our gear, made certain I got back to the room and on to the next event if I'd been out carousing. He said it made up for my providin' the truck and horse trailer to get us around, but he didn't have to do it. I was kind of lost without him there for a while, and sure enough, I left some of my things behind in a motel room. I got to the next meet and didn't have time to go back before my turn came with the bulls, so I figured what the hell, I could borrow a bull rope."

Pat O'Shea whistled through his teeth, and other men around the table who had ridden bulls murmured. Bodey pointed at the youth. "Never borrow someone else's bull rope."

"Oh, no, sir," the youth replied so earnestly that the older men laughed.

"I was four seconds out of the gate, and I came flyin' off that bull, got tangled in the borrowed rope. I swear that bull nearly turned himself inside out tryin' to get at me. He hooked me across the back. If the clowns and bullfighters hadn't gotten in his face, I'd be long gone. As it was, I nearly lost a kidney, was out eight weeks, finished so low in the rankings I thought they'd never let me ride again. Worst of all, my mama begged me to quit. Worked out all right, though. Sobered me up, and I came back a better man. The next year, I won my first All-Around. When Cody Lambert came up with the Kevlar protective vest, I was first in line to get one. Those things have saved some lives, and only a fool would ride without one now."

Telling the story helped Bodey clear his throat and distract Sarah Ann. "I was going to drive all night takin' the girls back to the Three B's, but after this fine meal, I might just fall asleep at the wheel. Could I put up here for the night?"

"I'll tell you what, Bodey. I'll fix up a guest room and let you have an extra helping of my peach cobbler with ice cream in exchange for an autographed picture," Sarah Ann said.

"The boys can put your heifers in a holding pen for the night. Won't be a problem," Pat O'Shea offered.

"I thank you. Just let me go get that picture. Two scoops, Sarah Ann," Bodey said as he pushed back from the table.

Out in an evening growing chill, Bodey rested his head against the truck's window. He had not a doubt in his mind that Pat O'Shea was his daddy. How did you tell a man he had a son over thirty years of age who'd been on his own for years? Bodey rummaged under the passenger seat for the envelope of signed pictures. He might be out of the game, but people still asked for them wherever he went.

Back in the kitchen, he personalized one of the

photos for Sarah Ann, "best cook west of the Sabine." To be honest, he thought Mama Tyne would be the best cook east of that river. The young hand shyly gave his name while the older men claimed to be getting the pictures for children and grandsons. Pat O'Shea said he was the last of his line and didn't have that excuse, so just make it out to him. Bodey did. He added "Glad to finally meet you."

As the group broke up for the evening, Bodey put a hand on O'Shea's wheelchair. "I could use some company out on the porch. It's a good night to watch the moon rise."

"Sure, I have some time. Sarah Ann says I need to get off my computer more. According to her, I should go into town and find a wife. Me." Pat shook his head doubtfully. "I used to be hell with the ladies a long time ago before the accident. Can't take them dancing anymore."

"My tastes ran the same way, but now I'm lookin' to settle down with a woman so fine she won't have none of me." Bodey took a seat on a porch rocker.

"That's how it goes, sometimes. What do they say, 'I wouldn't have any woman who'd have me'?"

"That's about right. Back in Lafayette all those years ago, do you remember meetin' a redheaded gal name of Betsy?" Bodey stared straight out into the night where the constellation Orion balanced on the edge of the horizon about to give place to the Scorpion rising in the night sky.

"I think I might. She wasn't the only girl I slept with on my last big fling, but got to say she was the best. I'm not braggin'. I was totally worthless back then. My daddy died when his tractor overturned. Ma

147

sold out and took me and my sister to the city. I couldn't stand the place. I left home when I turned seventeen, never finished high school, thought I was good enough to make a livin' on the circuit. I was just breaking into the big time when I drank and whored myself into a wheelchair. I'm sorry to say this if Betsy might be a relative of yours."

Bodey flinched at the word "whored." "She was my mother. Sarah Ann might be right about us being father and son. Bets, couldn't remember your name, just your Irish eyes. Then, you vanished off the circuit—your accident, I guess."

"I'm sorry," Patrick O'Shea said.

"For being my daddy?" The night deepened and made Bodey glad for the darkness.

"No, any man would be proud to own you. For being a disappointment to you, I guess. I'd like to think I would have helped out, been a father to you like Big Ben, but the truth is, I'm a better man now than I was then. You don't owe me a thing, not even an acknowledgment, but if you want to be sure, I'll take one of those blood tests."

"I'd like to know for sure. Bets swore you were Irish. She was right." Bodey gave a short laugh.

"There aren't more Irish names than Patrick O'Shea. The first one came over to help build the railroads. The family stayed in the west."

"So, I have an aunt?"

"In Fort Worth, and two female cousins near your age, one second cousin, and a grandma who is going to be overjoyed if this is true."

"From zero kin to five in a minute. It's hard to believe."

"None of your mama's folks are alive?"

"Just my grandparents who threw her out when she got pregnant and wouldn't give up her baby to a good Christian family. They're Baptists with the hardest of shells, so strict one son died of an overdose and the other committed suicide to get away from them, I think. The only times I met them were my high school and college graduations. The first time, they gave me a Bible, the second time, a gold cross. They said I'd need it if I planned to make a career out of rodeo. Even with Big Ben and Bets gone, I don't need that kind of people in my life. I aim to build my own family from scratch."

"Ever wear that cross?"

"Nope. I make my own luck."

"We all do, Bodey, but sometimes, I think there's more going on than we know or understand. I had no hope for a family, and you just made me a daddy at the age of fifty-four—son, if I can call you that. I want to introduce you to your kin soon as we know the truth about ourselves. They're good people. Hell, I'd be honored to introduce you even if I'm not your daddy, but hoping, even praying I am."

"Same goes here though I'm not too sure about the praying part. A couple of nuns implied I should do more of that if I want to reach the heart of a certain lady."

"Jesus God, I could have grandchildren someday. Don't deserve them of course. What do they say about God, that he has infinite mercy? If you won't pray, I'll do it for both of us, and light a few candles, too."

"Here I thought I was a non-practicing Baptist and turns out I'm Catholic in my bloodlines. Wait till I tell Eve."

Chapter Eleven

"Hey, honey. I'm home, darlin'."

Bodey stood in Eve's doorway greeting her the way he would a wife after a long business trip. Truth be told, he'd spent most of his adult life saying "so long" to women. Truth be told, he'd expected Eve to rush into his arms and give him a kiss.

Instead, she dropped her paintbrush, scowled. "Don't you ever knock? Gone two weeks, not a word, and now you don't even knock."

Bodey backed out the door and closed it behind him. He raised his fist to knock, but instead, the door flew open and Eve collided with his body flat on. Now this was more like it. Bodey put his arms around her and gave her the welcome home kiss he'd expected. Before he knew it, tongues got involved and his hands strayed up under the old shirt and beneath the sports bra where her soft, soft breasts peaked to hardness at the tips. One hand wandered down Eve's side and around her back where it plucked the bow from her braid and began unraveling her long, pale hair. Despite the shelter of the latticework, a truck full of teenage boys honked and hooted as they passed by on the blacktop.

Bodey backed Eve into the studio and kicked the door shut. Looking over her shoulder, he scanned the room for a likely place to lie down. The room seemed to be filled with nothing but easels and hard edges until he spotted the big drop cloth at the base of her Texas oak tree landscape. It didn't seem too cushy, but hell, he take the bottom position for her comfort. No problem there. He steered Eve around all obstacles toward the tarp. She'd gotten his shirt unbuttoned and was licking her way along his collarbone. When Bodey got to the cloth, he took them both to their knees, then did half a backwards roll to bring her up on top, far easier than flying from a bucking bull.

He yanked off her shirt and bra because he wanted to see those cream and pink breasts bobbing over him. He wanted to be able to reach up and grab and squeeze at any time during lovemaking. Eve, bless her heart, continued unbuttoning all the way to end of his fly. The second his erection sprang free, she mounted him, having nudged down her own leggings and whatever she wore under them. Wild ride ahead. Yippee! You go Miss Fancy Pants.

She rode him with her eyes closed and her head thrown back, a quick light sweat rising on her body like dew. Bodey clutched her hips and helped her rise and fall over him. As Eve came closer to her climax and he to his, she bent forward, her hair making a veil over them. He drew her close to his chest by gathering a hank in each fist and pumped his own hips upward. She gasped and moaned and kept on moving until a moment came when she froze over him, her mouth open in a silent scream. Bodey kept the rhythm until she lay, limp and still against him. He'd come with force a minute before her and was thankful he'd been able to see it through to the end like a successful bull ride.

Shivering with aftershocks, Eve rolled off of Bodey and huddled against the heat of his body. He wrapped a corner of the tarp over them, though he felt hot enough to give off steam. She laid her head over his heart and gloried in the tingling of her body all the way to the toes. What Eve wanted to do most was fall asleep, right here, right now, but the blood still singing through her body wouldn't allow it.

"Bodey, I'm a weak, weak woman."

"I wouldn't say that, honey. Let me tell you, your stamina is right up there with the best of 'em. I thought I was gonna pass out with so much of my blood racing to the bottom of my body."

"That's not what I meant. I went to confession on Friday and Mass this morning. I did my prayers, and I volunteered for six weeks of free art instruction at the Senior Center for that roll in the wisteria petals. I might as well make it six months and use up the credit."

"Sounds like a plan to me," Bodey answered with a self-satisfied grin.

Eve gave him a little slap on the cheek. "I'm serious. It bothers me that I have no restraint where you're concerned."

"Darlin', I might have teased about you being a Miss Fancy Pants years ago, but in my heart of hearts I think of you as my pure white convent rose. What we have together is great and no shame in that. Besides, I seriously asked you to marry me. You bolted out of my truck like a jackrabbit escapin' a coyote. Why was that?"

"A person shouldn't marry for lust. Because I keep thinking of being with you isn't a good reason to rush to the altar. I had a ten-year break from men and maybe that's all this is, a deluge after a dry spell. I just showed you I'm no pure white rose." Eve held up her hands soiled with spots of Indian red and cadmium yellow paint where she'd braced herself on the canvas when he drew her down.

"Lust is a time-honored reason to get married—along with a bun in the oven—and I don't think enjoying sex necessarily makes a woman impure." Bodey frowned. "Did we just have unprotected sex?"

"You're safe from becoming a daddy. I had my period while you were gone. In fact, it wasn't quite over."

"I wanted a yes or a no. No details, thanks. Besides, there are worse things than becoming a daddy, like never being one at all. That's what I came over here to tell you, but it went right out of my mind along with my blood supply. I found him. I found my father."

"Bodey, that's wonderful!" Eve caught herself. "Was it wonderful?"

"Actually, it was. His name is Patrick O'Shea, Irish just like Mama said. He oversees bookings and breeding operations on Connolly's ranch. He's also a paraplegic, had his spine crushed by a bull a week or so after he conceived me. That explains why he never came round on the rodeo circuit again. I guess he was sort of a rodeo bum before, and he says he's a better man now because of the accident. I believe him. I was late comin' back because I stayed to get acquainted. Then, we went over to Fort Worth and had a blood test taken to be sure. I met my grandma and aunt, some cousins."

Eve rose up beside him and looked into his eyes. Her genuine joy for him made his heart clench, and his view of her naked breasts made his dick twitch despite his total depletion. Give him a half hour and maybe.

"I'm so happy for you if it's true."

"He looks so much like me he could be my brother if he wasn't so old." Bodey pointed to his face. "The whole clan has these eyes."

"Now you're not alone."

"There's a difference between alone and lonely. A family in Fort Worth doesn't take care of the lonely." Bodey stroked Eve's hair and held her close. She shifted in his arms.

"Don't run off," he said.

"Bathroom," she answered.

"Oh, in that case, run."

He released her and watched while she tugged on enough clothes to pass through the courtyard with modesty. Bodey stretched and felt a twinge in his back. He got up more awkwardly than he would have liked and bent to straighten the drop cloth. Eve doubled over with a deep laugh. She pointed a finger.

"Paint spots. Veridian becomes you, and that blotch of alizarin crimson on your shoulder is better than a tattoo."

No matter which way he turned, he couldn't see the reasons for her hilarity. Eve laughed harder. Giving up, he shrugged. "This stuff wash off?"

"Yes, it's acrylic paint. Come with me. I'll wash your back."

"Now we're talkin', and when we're through in the bathroom, I'd like you to go back to the ranch with me and take a look at some livestock I bought."

"The mean cows? I'm no judge of cattle, Bodey," Eve answered, still laughing.

"Oh, I think you'll like this particular critter, but for now, let's check out your shower."

****

By the time Eve and Bodey learned that her tub was, indeed, big enough for two, they were sexually satiated and ravenously hungry. Eve made cheese omelets, which Bodey enhanced by dumping a half jar of salsa over his eggs. He finished off her carton of orange juice and took seconds on toast. Eve, he decided would make the best dessert, but she pushed him away.

"I thought you wanted to show me something at the ranch. It's getting dark, and I don't think I have enough food left for breakfast."

"No problem. There are lights in the barn, and if you stay over, I'll treat for breakfast."

"Let's just check out this mysterious critter for now."

They drove back to the Three B's in Bodey's truck. His headlights picked out the yellow forms of the three heifers in their small pasture as they passed. Bodey pulled in at the barn where he kept his horses. When he pushed open the door and flipped a light switch, Rocky thrust his head out of the stall and nickered.

Eve touched the horse's velvet nose. "When I saw you on this guy, I could have sworn you rode the same mount you had when you stopped me on the bridle trail my junior year at the Academy."

"This is his grandson, Rocky Three. The sequel is even better than the original version. Rocky Two is still standing stud at my place in Texas. What became of the dappled mare you were ridin' that day? She was finer than the usual trail horse. She belong to you?"

"My father gave me Dottie when I turned twelve so I could have my own horse here at the Academy. I couldn't afford to keep her after he vanished, so I donated her to the school. That's how they get most of their horses—from girls going off to college or moving on to better mounts. Sr. Nessy still used her to teach the little ones riding when I first came back here, but Dottie was past twenty. When the West Nile virus came around, she caught it and died. At least, I was with her at the end."

Bodey put a comforting arm around her shoulder. "You were a good rider. Dottie seemed a little skittish to me back when, but you had her under control the whole time."

"Your stud horse made her nervous. She was just scared. I always thought you would try to reach me again, but then, I heard about you and Renee."

"Well, Renee was givin' away what every teenage boy dreams about. Our fling didn't last out the summer."

They moved to the next stall where a sorrel gelding poked his head out and blinked his eyes in sleepy curiosity at the disturbance. Bodey scratched the quarter horse under its hairy chin. "This is Bullwinkle, my spare horse when I was on the circuit. Rocky hated getting in the trailer, but if old Bullwinkle went first, he'd go peacefully. They're buddies."

"What, you couldn't find a name from the Rocky movies?" Eve joked.

"Bullwinkle may be a gelding, but it still would have been an insult to call him Adrienne."

They reached a third stall, and Eve sighed softly. "Oh, isn't she beautiful."

A yearling filly pricked her shiny black ears at the sound. She shifted, showing them a white rump that looked as if it had been covered with lacy snowflakes.

Two white socks on her hind feet and a star on her forehead made her even more showy.

"I think that is the prettiest Appaloosa I've ever seen. What's her name?" Eve held out an open hand to coax the filly to her.

"My new-found daddy and me, we killed some time at a livestock show in Dallas. We both thought she'd be a good investment. I'll train her myself. She had another name, but now she is officially Three B's Miss Fancy Pants, Fancy for short."

Eve gave her throaty laugh. "How perfect!"

"Yeah, that's what I called you when you shot me down back when we were kids. I thought you were perfect, too."

"I'd be insulted if you hadn't added that last part. You must have figured out by now I'm hardly perfect." The filly edged closer and licked Eve's palm with her broad tongue.

"Still way too good for me even with a new found daddy."

Eve answered by taking his face in her hands and initiating a kiss. She ran her hands over the evening stubble on his cheeks and up into the thickness of his dark hair. The yearling stuck her nose between them snuffling for treats. Bodey backed Eve toward an open stall, then thought the better of it.

"No, once a day on the floor is enough. We're going to bed, my bed—and I'd carry you there if I didn't have a bum knee."

Laughing, Eve led the way.

Chapter Twelve

"Wake up, Miss Fancy Pants!" Bodey's voice boomed in Eve's ear. He gave her a playful swat on the rear. "We have time for a ride before breakfast, and it's a glorious mornin' out there."

"I don't seem to be wearing *any* pants," Eve said sleepily. She yawned and stretched, then realized Bodey had ripped the sheet off her naked body and was enjoying the show entirely too much. Eve curled into a ball covered mostly by her hair. "You're very pleased with yourself today. What time is it?"

"Six-thirty in the a.m. The horses are saddled and ready to go. I figure you need to learn to ride western style if you're gonna be livin' on a ranch."

Too groggy to argue, Eve stumbled into the bathroom and shut the door. She washed her face with cold water and used a warm, soapy cloth between her legs, not that Bodey or the horse would care. She twisted her own long mane into a single braid and secured it with rubber bands at the top and bottom. This was going to be a morning without makeup. She expected to see the face of woman over thirty and badly in need of concealer when she looked in the mirror, but the face staring back had shining eyes, pink cheeks, and a smile on her face. All the little lines seemed to have vanished under the glow of happiness.

Eve found the worn jeans and faded pink T-shirt

she'd thrown on for a night visit to the Three B's stable when she'd had no intention of staying over and covered her body. She searched for the old sneakers with holes in the toes that she'd kicked off somewhere in the bedroom.

"Don't bother. You need boots." Bodey threw open his closet. "We may have to stuff the toes with something."

Eve looked astounded. "How many pairs of boots do you have?"

"Oh, I don't know. Maybe fifty. A lot of them are promotional items companies pay me to wear. Good thing Big Ben had almost as many, or I wouldn't have all these nice slots to put them in." Bodey took a pair from the rack and gave them a sniff. "These have never been worn—because I wouldn't caught dead in 'em. Too rhinestone cowboy for me. You keep 'em when we're done with our lesson."

The boots were white and had elaborate gold stitching forming roses on the sides. Eve tried them on. Not a bad fit at all, but a shock that she had feet nearly as big as his and a few inches on him in height when he didn't wear boots, not all that often really. She felt a self-deprecating need to point this out. "I guess you've noticed my feet aren't exactly dainty."

"Honey, I never noticed your feet at all. We're about the same height when I have my boots and hat on so it goes to figure."

Eve regarded herself in the mirror. "If I had spangles across my chest, I could be taken for a University of Texas drum majorette."

"Now we're talkin'. Remind me to buy you the whole outfit someday. Come on now, Rocky and

Bullwinkle are waitin'.'"

Bodey had tied the two horses by the kitchen door. He let Eve grab a cup of freshly brewed coffee and a slightly stale Danish on the way out. She finished her impromptu breakfast while Bodey gave her riding instructions.

"Remember you neck-rein a western horse, put pressure on the side opposite of where you want to go. It's not so much about tuggin' on the bit unless you want to stop."

Eve sat her coffee mug down on the edge of a flowerbed. "Let's give it a try then." She grasped the horn, put a foot in the low-hanging stirrup, and swung a leg over the saddle. "Hey, I can mount up myself, but I feel like my legs are dangling."

"No, I got the stirrups about right for you. Give the Bull some boot and away we go."

Eve kicked her mount's side and woke him from an early morning doze. Bodey steered Rocky alongside Bullwinkle, and they ambled by the fence line for a mile or two admiring the dawn and the blooming white Cherokee roses that had taken over since Big Ben's time. Bodey got down and unlatched a gate into a pasture where placid Black Angus cows with three-month-old calves by their sides were spread out grazing on the spring grass.

"Let's pick up the speed some. And none of that up and down posting stuff. Just hang on with your knees and enjoy the ride."

Bodey let Eve go ahead. When they reached the far end of the field, Bodey increased the pace, and they galloped around the perimeter upsetting the mama cows who called to their young to huddle at their side and bunch up into a herd.

"Want to have some fun? We can cut a few cows," Bodey suggested.

"That sounds cruel."

"From the herd, Eve, not with a knife. How did I end up with a city girl like you? Show ole Bullwinkle which pair you want and go after 'em, but watch out for sudden moves."

Bullwinkle for all this lackadaisical air when he was standing still went after the cow and her baby like a hound dog after a coon. He pushed the bawling animals away from the herd and countered their every attempt to return to the group with his neck snaked out and a steady eye on the quarry. The gelding drove them toward the gate where Bodey waited. When Eve finally pulled him up and allowed the frantic cow to go back to her friends, she felt as if she'd just been along for the ride.

"Well, what an experience for both me and the cow," she gasped.

"You didn't lose your seat. You'll do just fine on a ranch."

"Bodey, let's not assume anything right now."

Eve led the way back to the barns where she unsaddled and groomed her own horse beside Bodey and Rocky. After letting the horses out for grass, Eve heaved the heavy saddle off the side of the stall where she'd placed it and asked Bodey where it belonged.

"Tack room's over here." He opened the door with a flourish.

Eve blinked. The spacious room was festooned with glossy pictures of Bodey riding bulls and broncos. Ornate unused prize saddles sat on forms against the far wall. Gold buckles filled a glass case. Gaudy chaps embossed with enough endorsements for a NASCAR racer spread out as wall hangings along with an assortment of braided ropes and cow bells. The place smelled of new leather and old, as well as dust from the rodeo ring.

"Ah, where should I put this?" Eve said of the plain, practical saddle she held.

"The workin' stuff goes up front, right there by you."

Eve relieved herself of the saddle and took another step into the room. "You've accomplished a lot since you left Rainbow, Bodey."

"Got more of this stuff at my place in Texas."

Eve moved to the back of the room and fingered the braided ropes. "And these are…?"

"My favorite bull ropes. Let me show you how they work." Bodey took down one of the straps and hung a cowbell from it. He tied it around Eve's body and let the bell dangle down between her legs. Slowly, he backed her up against one of the prize saddles.

Eve swore she could feel the cold of the metal bell through her clothes pressing against the parts of her that were growing hot. Eyes closed, she arched back over the saddle. With a single tug, Bodey released the bull rope. The bell fell to the floor with a clank, and her jeans followed it. Eve stayed spread-legged where she was. Bodey picked up a loose end of the rope and rubbed it lightly back and forth between her thighs until she moaned. He unbuckled and dropped his own pants down to his ankles, at this point no sense in doing anything more. He pushed inside of Eve, and she bucked against him. He rode her hard to the end until they were both draped across the saddle more or less holding each other up.

"Still think we ain't compatible, Miss Fancy Pants?" Bodey asked, feeling his heart pumping hard the way it did after his best rides.

"I think I'm willing to give this relationship a try, cowboy, but I do have conditions."

Chapter Thirteen

Here they sat again at the eleven o'clock Mass on Sunday, attendance being one of Eve's conditions for continuing their relationship. The church meant a great deal to her, and she'd expect him to convert and raise any children they might have in the religion. Honest to God, Bodey didn't think he'd ever be much of a churchgoer, regardless of his Irish genes. The Catholic church had way too much upping and downing, singing and standing in line for dry, papery wafers, not that he and Eve had been doing that last part. She'd skipped confession ever since Bodey returned from Texas with the mean cows, a fact the canny old nuns obviously noticed but did not mention. Still, Eve dragged him to Mass where he often dozed off during the sermon, especially if they had been up all night making love.

Across the aisle, Rusty Niles smirked at his friend as they hit the kneelers yet again, Noreen and Jesse in perfect unison with him, and little Katie stashed in a nursery somewhere. Bodey closed his eyes. He had only one thing to pray for, that Eve would accept his second proposal, so he concentrated on that goal during the quiet times when he wasn't required to mumble along with some hymn or recite a creed.

Time and prayer, the old nuns had told him. They continued to repeat this advice at the café's Sunday buffet where he took them each week at Eve's insistence. This should have been awkward on the Sundays Eve worked the tables, but not really. The Sisters, at least Sr. Nessy, could talk horses. Both had charming stories to relate about Eve's time at the Academy, and some not-so-charming things to tell about her family, though this news to Bodey was never said in an ugly way.

More like, "Eve's father doted on her, of course, not a good thing for a young woman. At least, her mother had enough wisdom to place Eve here where she could develop some character regardless of family circumstances. But, Eve's mother wasn't so much wise as non-maternal, not a nurturer, willing to leave her daughter's upbringing to others."

"Too busy nurturing her resentments against the father, I'd say." Sr. Inez put it bluntly.

"You shouldn't say, Sister. I've often wondered about the father, though. Did he really die at sea? No, no, he loved Eve too much to desert her." Sr. Helen raised a bite of pecan pie to her lips on a trembling fork. Lent had passed, and Easter come and gone during Bodey's stay in Texas.

The Sisters, Bodey realized, made up Eve's family now, much as if they were two beloved maiden aunts. He treated them kindly and learned all he could to understand Eve. His own now confirmed daddy approved of Bodey's choice for a wife, too, once he had been pried from the bull-raising business and coaxed for a visit.

Watching Bodey work with Miss Fancy Pants, the woman, not the horse, Patrick said, "You can see she's quality. She has an inborn gentleness and style."

When Eve called them to come in for a dinner she

had put together from Bodey's meager groceries, Pat waved her way and added, "That's quality, too, son. Good choice."

The recessional blared on the organ and jolted Bodey from his reverie. He stood and followed Eve out into the May sunshine. The temperature stood in the mid-eighties, and he thought Eve might enjoy a swim after her shift at the café. He could rub down her white skin with lotion and…

"Bodey, would you help Sr. Helen to my car? I want to tell Amanda and Hardy we'll be coming to their renewal ceremony next week. I won't be long." Eve hurried off to catch the couple who walked arm-in-arm followed by all four children, eighteen, sixteen, fourteen, and twelve, son, daughter, son, daughter.

Bodey put on the white Stetson that had been taking up a place on the pew and flipped a pair of sunglasses over his eyes. He offered an arm to Sr. Helen and watched Eve speak to Hardy. Red Courville gave not one hint that he had ever hit on his woman. Red smiled and drew his wife closer.

Rusty, his arms holding copper-curled Katie, sidled up to Bodey. Clearly, he was cracking up at seeing the great Bodey Landrum with two elderly nuns on his arms instead of a couple of rodeo buckle bunnies. Their creeping procession halted when the Sisters indicated they wanted to speak to Noreen. Young Jesse, bored, bolted off to play in a nearby fountain despite his mother's shouted warning not to get wet.

"My, my, my, six weeks straight attendance at Mass. You gonna keep that up after you marry Eve?" Russ chafed. "Course, you'll have to set a good example for the dozen kids Eve wants."

"I don't know about Mass. I'm not sure Eve will have me. She stays over some nights, but sitting next to her in church is about as much of her company as I get, otherwise. She has her ridin' lessons, her art classes, her commissions to work on, and her waitressing. I keep sayin' she should move in with me, save her rent, and give up the job at the Rainbow Café, but I honestly think she's worried about what the nuns might say. And who said anything about a dozen kids? I'd like some, sure, but a dozen?" Bodey shook his head.

"Here, get some practice."

Rusty handed over Katie, whose fingers were a sticky red from some I've-been-good-in-Sunday-school treat. She went right for Bodey's hat. He whipped it off and held it down near the ground with his free hand. Katie protested with a wail.

"Oh, for heaven's sake, don't torment Bodey with the baby, Russ. You know he isn't used to children," Noreen fussed, breaking off her conversation with the nuns. "Go get your son out of that fountain."

Taking Katie back, Rusty whispered, "Walk along. It seems Cousin Renee told her mama over the phone that Eve scared off that artist fellow by telling him she wanted nothing less than marriage and a big family, a dozen kids at least. Renee, on the other hand, has found her calling in being Evan's muse. I think that means she's posing nekkid for him. She sold a few of her own pictures, too. There's a huge market for male nudes in San Francisco, evidently."

"I don't doubt it," Bodey answered. "Eve never mentioned wanting children, let alone how many, just that I should get used to going to church and being nice to nuns." He frowned. "Why would she tell Evan and not me?"

"Who knows?" Rusty pulled his son up by the collar of a white church-going shirt wet to the elbows. The knees of the boy's khaki pants were stained a mossy green. "Your mom doesn't want you swimming in front of the church, boy. Maybe Uncle Bodey will invite you over to use his pool this afternoon. It's hot enough."

"You're welcome to come, Jesse, all of you. Eve won't be free till around three. Maybe she could bring some ribs over, or I'll throw some steaks on the grill."

"Sounds good, buddy. We'll come over around two. Noreen will bring some sides, beans or something." With the group reassembled, the Niles family moved toward their SUV.

"Bye-bye, Unc Bodey." Katie, red curls bobbing, waved over her daddy's shoulder.

Troubled, Bodey helped the nuns into Eve's Toyota and rode shotgun to the Café. As usual, he helped the Sisters with their plates while Eve hurried to the back to slip into her waitressing clothes. Settled at a table, Bodey, scowling, pushed his corn *maque choux* into his smothered potatoes and stirred them together. He took a bite and put down his fork.

"Sisters, do you think Eve wants to have a family some day?"

"Certainly. I don't think she'll ever join our order now," Sr. Inez answered.

Bodey had the grace to look embarrassed, but he wasn't easily put off. "She ever say anything about wantin' a dozen kids?"

The nuns appeared startled. "Eve is getting a bit old to try for that many children, but whatever the Lord sends," Sr. Helen said carefully.

"Why wouldn't she tell me somethin' like that?"

"Time and prayer, Bodey." Sr. Inez flew back to that old advice like a crow to a corn crib. It seemed other little birdies released into the wild were coming home to roost, too.

"But how much time and how much prayer?" Bodey asked.

"Lord knows," said Sr. Helen.

Chapter Fourteen

The week before the Courville's renewal ceremony, Eve had an opening at a gallery in Dallas. Bodey felt he had been of some use to her there. For one thing, he'd gone over all her prices and doubled them.

"Honey, if you don't do this, you won't have nothin' left once the gallery takes its thirty percent of any sales," he advised. He had a head for business. Eve, like many artists, did not. Not that he'd ever say those words aloud, but he did point out her notecards should be ten dollars a pack, not five, especially in Dallas where things weren't valued unless overpriced.

Now, he was doing his best for her at the reception by standing near his portrait, which had been arrestingly hung on a short wall space between icons of the angels, Michael and Gabriel. He supposed the colors complemented his picture because he sure wasn't anyone's guardian angel. Bodey took a sip of the sour white wine, crunched his Havarti cheese and water crackers, and waited for someone to notice him. Finally, the arts reporter saw the resemblance and had her photographer take a snapshot. Bodey supplied her with a quote. "I plan to buy this likeness of myself. It will be my second Eve Burns. She is highly collectible, and this ole cowboy will fit in just right with my holdings in western art."

His art buyer spouted stuff like this when he wanted Bodey to make a purchase. Regardless, Bodey turned down the things he thought were butt ugly or totally incomprehensible. After that, he got one of the gallery attendants to red dot his portrait and went forth to mingle.

Eve framed the doorway to the larger display space with two of her big icons, one of the Virgin and Child and another of St. Paul, but once inside, Eve's landscapes filled the walls with the Texas oak tree mural dominating the rear of the room. The mural, appropriately labeled *The Glory of Texas*, belonged to the collection of Mr. and Mrs. Frances "Frank" Huntington the label noted. Mrs. Got Rocks stood nearby to interpret her commission to anyone who couldn't figure out the scenes of Texas, past and present, and to inform everyone her mural had larger dimensions than the one in Lafayette, as it should be. Eve posed in her borrowed black dress with her patron for the society page photographer.

Bored beyond calculation, Bodey wandered toward the exit. He thought he'd seen a good barbecue place down the block when they arrived. Instead, he bumped into a cluster of women entering dressed in their Sunday best as opposed to artsy black or Texas rich couture. The small white-haired woman in the center of the group scanned the gathering of drifting art lovers.

"Grandma, you came!" Bodey lifted the little lady off her feet and twirled her around.

Blue eyes sparkling, the elderly woman regained her balance and pecked Bodey's cheek. "We would have been here sooner, but traffic was terrible, and no parking to be found at all. We had to walk from a lot four blocks away. Now, let me meet this Eve you are so fond of." Elsie O'Shea made it clear from the start that art was not her purpose for going to so much trouble, though she did pause to admire the icons and Bodey's portrait.

"Eve." Bodey separated her neatly from a conversation with a man who reminded him too much of Hardy Courville like a cowboy on a good cutting horse. "I'd like you to meet my grandma, Elsie O'Shea, my Aunt Bridget Cochran, and her daughters Shannon and Chloe."

"I'm so pleased that you came." Eve pressed the arthritic hand of Elsie O'Shea gently as she would those of the elderly nuns.

"You painted all these holy pictures, did you? And Bodey half-naked," Grandma O'Shea asked.

"Or half-clothed as the case may be. Guilty, but you should have seen the other artist's interpretation of your grandson." Eve laughed and let her eyes rove toward Bodey.

"Pick out your favorite. I want you to have one of Eve's paintings," Bodey insisted.

"We hardly met, and he wanted to be buying me a new car and a house, but I said I was happy in my little apartment, and it's rare that I drive anymore. Still, a holy picture would be a fine thing to have. Those angels are mighty handsome fellows. What do you think, Bridget? Gabriel or Michael?"

"Both," said Bodey.

"I'll give you a special price," Eve replied.

"No special prices, I keep tellin' you. I see the big Virgin sold and some of your small landscapes."

"Yes, evidently someone has been passing the

word that I am highly collectible."

"That so?" Bodey preened. "Glad to hear the gallery workers are doing their jobs. You ladies want something to eat? All they got here is cheese, grapes, and a wine they must have bought at a convenience store, but I'll take y'all for barbecue when this shindig is over."

Bridget and her girls moved toward the meager refreshment table. Mrs. O'Shea would not to be lured away by drink and crackers.

"So, you come from Rainbow, Louisiana, the town where miracles happen?"

"I've lived there for the past ten years and graduated from the Academy. As for miracles, I can't say I've seen any."

"Oh, but you have. Bodey moved to Rainbow, and in a few months he found the father he's been looking for these many years. That was surely a miracle for my Patrick. I feared he might kill himself after his accident, he got so low. I kept saying, you might never know what good things life will bring you if you aren't around to see. Later, he thought that was getting the education he ran away from and having a job he loves, but all along Bodey waited for him."

"I suppose you could see a divine hand in that," Eve said neutrally.

"And then, consider my best friend, Maydell Folse. She went to Rainbow on a retreat, her arthritis so bad she couldn't kneel in prayer and beseeched the Blessed Mother Leontine to give her some relief. The next week the FDA approved a new drug that gave her back almost her full range of motion. Miracles, my dear, aren't always announced by apparitions or angels.

Sometimes, it's the FDA."

Eve swallowed a chuckle along with a sip of cheap wine. "Who am I to say it's not?" she replied. When the gallery owner towed her away to meet a potential client, Eve gratefully fled her tiny interrogator.

Elsie O'Shea eyed the short, black dress and loose blonde hair as Eve swayed away. "Not after your money, now, is she, Bodey?"

"I keep offerin' it to her, but she keeps pushing it back—like some other woman I know who turned down a new car and a nicer place to live."

Holding little plastic plates of fruit and cheese, his new female relatives regrouped around Bodey. "What do y'all think of my girl?" he asked them.

"Gorgeous," answered Chloe. "I wish I had hair like that and legs so long."

"Love her dress," said Shannon.

"Very talented," replied Aunt Bridget.

"But is she a good Catholic girl, Bodey?" Grandma Elsie asked. "She doesn't seem to believe in miracles."

"Well, she drags me to Mass every Sunday, Grandma."

"That's good, then. She cares for your soul, and probably your body, too, judging by that picture, but she seems a bit fancy to make a ranch wife. I loved my husband and followed him where he needed to be, but once he was gone, I couldn't wait to get back to the city, and I came from much humbler stock than her."

"My small spread in Rainbow would hardly be called a ranch by Texas standards, and that's where I plan to live with Eve. Mama had a sunroom that would make her a good studio for now, and I could build her a bigger place later. It's not like I'd be askin' Eve to cook for the hands or stay up nights with colicky calves."

"I suppose it might work, but don't get your hopes up or your heart broken, my only grandson." Elsie gave Bodey a butterfly light pat on the cheek.

When the opening closed, Bodey herded his women to the barbecue dive where they gorged on pulled pork sandwiches and fresh cut French fries heavy with grease. He saw his new relations back to their car, and escorted Eve to the hotel where he'd booked a suite.

"Too tired?" he asked Eve when he had her lying on fresh white sheets, her blonde hair spread across the pillow. He ran a tanned hand down her pale body all the way to the cleft between her legs. She shivered.

"No. I feel like celebrating."

Bodey leaned over to take her breast in his mouth.

"Bodey?"

He nodded his head to show he was listening.

"What did your new family think of me?"

He sighed and fell back on the pillow next to her.

"Don't stop," Eve said.

"Can't talk with my mouth full. Let's see, you are gorgeous and talented. Grandma likes that you go to Mass, but is worried that you don't believe in miracles."

"I could have used one when my father, and then my mother died, and my boyfriend left me, and the bills piled up. I prayed for one, but as the years passed, I came to believe what Sr. Helen once said to me. God gave me the talent and the strength to see me through, and I would have to be content with that."

"What would be a real miracle to you?"

"Oh, I don't know anymore. You found your

daddy. Maybe mine would be having my father back to walk me down the aisle at my wedding."

"I can't make that happen, honey, and you won't let me pay off your bills, but if you'd just hush, I'd like to do a little miracle workin' of my own. The dead has been raised down there, and he wants to come home to paradise."

Chapter Fifteen

Everyone attending declared the renewal ceremony of Amanda and Hardy Courville to be a beautiful and heartfelt occasion. Amanda wore a white lace dress underlaid with gold in a style less tailored than usual, and her two daughters, also in white, served as her attendants. Hardy lined up with his two sons, all in matching gray suits. When Hardy departed from the standard ceremony to announce loudly that he would worship his wife with his body all the days of their lives, all four teenagers cringed while their mother blushed and smiled. The priest, shaken and wordless for a moment, managed to gain his composure and finish the ceremony, but generally all the witnesses enjoyed the comment, especially Bodey who whispered to Eve that he'd like to say the same if he ever got around to marrying.

The bridal party recessed down the aisle of the nun's chapel with the Courville rose window and the Niles side windows throwing jewels of color on them as the strong May sunlight streamed through their panels. Amanda and Hardy paused to pose for a photograph under an arbor draped in pure, white roses shedding their petals like summer snow in the heat. Those roses reminded Bodey of Eve. Noreen and Rusty always went on about their special flower, a small yellow blossom named the Courville rose after her family and common as dirt around Rainbow, but seldom found elsewhere. Rusty had courted Noreen with a nosegay of them. While Bodey pointed out just how gay he thought that was back when he was a teenager, he saw the use of such a gesture now.

He leaned toward Eve who watched the scene with a smile on her pale pink lips and joy in her gray eyes for the reunited couple, not one bad thought or ill wish sent Hardy's way for his transgressions. Bodey thought the man got off easy. He whispered to Eve, "That's your flower, a pure white convent rose. That's how I think of you. I want to plant them all over my ranch."

"You already have lots of white Cherokee roses growing in the ditches."

"But, they are common and thorny, nothing like you." He laid it on as best a cowboy could.

"Oh Bodey, right now I'm more like that wisteria grove, all tangled up inside and gone wild."

"That's fine with me, too. We can grow both at the Three B's, children, too. Just how many did you say you wanted? Because I can give 'em to you."

"Stop it! This isn't the time or the place. Let's get out of the sun."

Okay, so more time and more prayer. Bodey snorted like a frustrated bull and followed Eve to the refreshments. The heat and humidity drove the guests directly to the shade of white tents set up on the lawn and into the care of the caterer's assistants offering trays of chilled champagne and fruit punch. Lines formed to fill plates with cucumber and shrimp salad finger sandwiches and tiny puff pastry cups of crawfish etouffee. The renewal feast was as dainty and tasteful as the bride herself.

Bodey and Eve watched the cutting of a full-sized wedding cake, white with a raspberry filling. Bodey shifted around unhappily, loosening his shirt collar with a finger.

"What's the matter? Missing cold beer and potato chips?" Eve asked.

"And a good ball game on TV, too. I figure if I eat a dozen of these, it might make a meal." Bodey popped the last pastry cup on his plate into his mouth and swallowed. "Red Courville gets on my nerves sometimes, tellin' people he had those flowers flown all the way in from New York for his bride and invitin' all the tourists and gawkers in for cake.

"Lily of the valley doesn't grow here, so it's special."

"No kiddin'. Any minute now one of those strangers is gonna ask for my autograph, and we'll be here all afternoon. Here comes one now dressed up like the captain on *Gilligan's Island* and lookin' like him, too."

Eve turned her head to where Bodey gestured, but the big-bellied man in the nautical hat and blue blazer veered aside and headed for the restrooms. "Not a fan of rodeo, I guess," she remarked wryly.

Amanda Courville did approach them, however, floating over the grass in her high-waisted gown. "Eve, I want you to have this bouquet. I have a confession to make, and this glorious day is the right time. I thought once you and Hardy were having an affair. Why, at the art opening, he didn't even ask me to stand with him at the unveiling. I was inside 'making things nice for Eve' like a good wife. I barely spoke to you that evening."

"Think nothing of it. A lot was going on that night,

179

too much." Eve raised the hand-tied bouquet of lily of the valley to her nose and sniffed the heady fragrance of the tiny belled flowers.

"But then, I looked over to where Hardy stood talking to the Sisters, and suddenly, it was as if he saw me for the first time in years."

Tears welled up in Amanda's eyes. Bodey whipped out a clean handkerchief from his suit pocket and shoved it her way. Women crying made him want to run in the opposite direction. She could keep the hankie, or did they call them pocket squares now?

"So sorry, I've been weepy lately." Amanda dabbed her eyes carefully and lowered her voice. "It's the baby. Can you believe, forty-two and expecting a fifth child? Hardy is very excited about it. I think—I think it happened that night at the art opening when we went back into the office." Her cheeks suffused with a delicate pink.

Speaking of the devil, Red Courville broke into their group and put his arm around Amanda. He offered her a flute of bubbling beverage.

"Sparkling cider for the little mother. She told you, didn't she? I don't even want to know which sex it is since we got two of both. This one just seals the deal as far as I'm concerned. Makes the day even happier."

"Congratulations." Bodey offered his hand. "Y'all got a great wife and a baby on the way. You take good care of 'em, now."

"Eve, I'd like to commission one of your Virgin and child icons to celebrate this birth. As for you two, I hope it works out." Amanda nodded toward the bouquet in Eve's hand. "Oh, I see Sr. Helen and Sr. Inez over there. Hardy, we must speak to them."

"Absolutely. Those old—holy ladies showed me I already had the best woman on earth. No offense, Eve."

"None taken, Hardy. Tell the Sisters we'll be coming to visit shortly."

As Hardy and Amanda moved away, Eve caught a glimpse of the man in the blue blazer and captain's hat ducking behind the four-tiered wedding cake slowly being disassembled into slices by the caterer. "Your fan is back, Bodey. It looks like he's too afraid to come over here."

"His problem, then. I don't want to get a line started. Look here..." He dug in his coat pocket and withdrew some folded newspaper clippings. "Grandma sent these for you from the Dallas paper last Sunday, front page of the Arts section. Great pictures of you and me and a good review, too."

Eve skimmed the article and smiled. "Not raves, but some nice comments. 'Eve Burns manages to imbue even her static icons with her serene spirit which spills over even more noticeably into her landscapes.' 'Judging by the one example of famous bull rider, Bodey Landrum, Burns could have made a career as a portrait artist as well.' Tell, your grandmother I really appreciate her sending this along."

"Let me get it framed for you," Bodey offered.

"Uh-oh, here comes your fan, sort of hiding behind one of the wedding programs he picked up. Why don't you just go sign it for him and get it over with?"

"Guy looks familiar. You know him?"

"I doubt it—wait! Bodey, that's my father, older, his hair all turned white and much heavier, but it's him, really him."

"Well then, I guess we'd better go over and say

hello."

Bodey took Eve's arm and felt her trembling. The man had pulled his cap down. Only a pair of white brows and gray eyes showed between the brim and the program. As they approached, the mystery guest moved from the tent, and looking around, went back to the chapel. Eve and Bodey followed, bursting into the cool, air-conditioned sanctuary on a blast of hot air from outside.

Eve's father waited for them in the last pew. He held out his arms. "Princess, I'm back, but if your mother sees me, she'll have me dead and buried, then take all my money."

Seeing Eve's stricken face, Bodey gave him the news. "Your ex-wife is the one dead and buried these last ten years, Mr. Burns. Cancer got her, and she left Eve with a mountain of bills that still aren't paid off." Eve might be thrilled to see the man, but Bodey didn't plan on letting him off easy like Hardy Courville.

"Well, she wasn't my responsibility anymore," Burns claimed, and seeing Bodey's look of disgust added, "Of course, I would have helped my baby out if I'd been around."

"Yeah, fathers are supposed to take care of their kids. Husbands are supposed to be true to their wives. Doesn't always work out that way, and words are cheap."

"Bodey, please, he's here now. Dad, where have you been? How did you find me?"

Dickie Burns withdrew a newspaper clipping from his pants pocket. "Fellow named Huntington left a Dallas paper on my boat. Said he'd done his wife's art opening and deserved a week off to go after marlin.

There you were, all grown up, a real artist, and pretty as a princess. I wanted to see you, tell you how proud I am of you. Just a quick trip to the mainland. I go by Rich Kuhl now. Get it, Dickie Burns becomes Rich Kuhl."

"Clever," said Bodey sourly. "It's my guess you had money stashed in an offshore account to keep you all these years."

"Safe from my creditors and the IRS, yes. Killed me to scuttle the Princess Eve, though. She was a beautiful ship, beautiful like my only daughter. I could have ended up in jail. You understand, baby?" Rich asked his child, taking her hands in his.

"I suppose. I wish you had let me know you were alive."

"Your mother would have turned me in if you ever let it slip. Even now, I can't stay here. What I want is for you to come back to the islands with me. I have a nice place near the beach on a small cay, a good business going, four charter boats and lots of cheap labor. You can paint all you want. No more waitressing for my princess."

"You know about that?"

"Rainbow has always been a small town, whiter now than it used to be. I stopped by that pottery place, and the woman told me you'd either be at the café working or up at the chapel for a friend's party. They pointed out your house to me. It's cute, but nothing like what I have in the islands. So how about it?"

"You come back here after nearly fourteen years after Eve has struggled to pay off her mother's bills and make something of herself, and you want her to hold out her arms and say all is forgiven? At least my daddy had a real excuse. But this, this is all a big pile of bullshit, and I do know bullshit when I see it." Bodey spun his dress Stetson on one hand to keep from reaching out and flattening Eve's old man.

Rich Kuhl stared at the spinning hat and the toes of Bodey's boots. "Who the hell is this cowboy? Tell him to go away, Princess, and let us alone."

Eve pointed to the smaller picture in the clipping. "He's Bodey Landrum, four times All-Around Cowboy, five times World Champion Bull Rider."

"Yeah," Rich sneered. "I know all about Bodey Landrum, Betsy Barnum's bastard kid. Big Ben, when he'd had a few, told me even Bets didn't know who the boy's daddy was. This cowboy went out to the barn on his eighteenth birthday to screw some slut from the Academy—like father, like son—and that girl just like his mama. He thought he was hot shit back then, swimming in Barnum's money and never having to lift a finger unless he wanted to fuck a schoolgirl. How'd you ever get mixed up with him?"

Just like that, the years rolled back and Bodey was nothing more than Big Ben's charity case stepson. More years slipped away, and his mama worked at the diner, packing his school lunches from restaurant leftovers so her son wouldn't be teased about getting free food from the government.

The pain came on so swiftly, wiping out all of his adult accomplishments that Bodey threw his hat down and shot out his fist. Eve got in the way. He couldn't pull his punch fast enough to avoid striking the bare, white flesh of her upper arm. She'd have a bruise. He knew it, regretted his action immediately.

"For God's sake, Bodey, we're in a church, and this is my father."

"And God knows he's a fraud, and I'm the real deal. Yeah, well, I'm leavin' now. When you figure out if you're moving to the islands with this sad sack of cow crap, you let me know." Bodey stalked out and tried to slam the chapel doors, but instead, they shut silently behind him on well-oiled hinges.

Chapter Sixteen

Bodey felt the same urgency he'd had when Hardy Courville and Evan Adams were competing with him for Eve's attention. Only this time her father presented much tougher competition, a man who called her "Princess" and had a childhood of happy memories to draw upon, getting in his way. When the call came Monday morning that the ring he'd ordered was ready, he drove immediately to Lafayette to collect it from Jason Roth, an Art Guild member who designed his own jewelry. So pleased with the work, he topped Roth's fee by twenty percent.

Inside the jeweler's velvet box glowed an amethyst stone the size of his thumb tip and of a ripe and delicious deep purple hue. Two platinum clusters of molded wisteria blooms held the jewel in place. Engraved tendrils and sprays of ragged leaves decorated the band. Eve's hands were long-fingered, large, and capable. She could show off a designer piece like this with no trouble at all the designer assured him.

This was the kind of ring Eve would want, not some ten-carat extravaganza from a fancy retail shop. Rusty, wise in the ways of women, had once told Bodey that special women deserved and desired unique objects meant only for them. Noreen wore an engagement ring of gold and rubies, a family heirloom, out of style, but totally in keeping with that woman's strange belief she and Rusty were soul mates and the reincarnated spirits of past lovers. If he'd had the time to show Russ the wisteria ring, Bodey knew his best friend would say Bodey Landrum had finally gotten things right. Glad he hadn't gone with a diamond and a rose design since that compliment seemed to annoy and distress Eve, Bodey shut the box with a satisfying snap and dropped it in his jacket pocket.

He wanted to get this proposal just right, too. He'd go to Mama Tyne and get a special picnic lunch. They'd ride to the wisteria grove. The glade would be shady and pleasant this time of year. After they had eaten and made love, he'd propose again, the right way, down on his bum knee if necessary. She wouldn't bolt this time. He knew it would work—if her newly returned father hadn't poisoned her against him.

First things, first. He drove over to Eve's house to set the date into motion. Her school classes were over for the summer, her students gone home. She hadn't called to nag him into going to church on Sunday, too wrapped up in Daddy, no doubt. Eve might be teaching her old lady artists today, but it would only take a minute to set up the date for lunch, and he knew she wasn't working tonight. If she said yes, why hell, she could even have her father walk her down the aisle despite Bodey's dislike of the old man. He could swallow it for one day so long as Eve didn't run off to the islands with that pitiful excuse for a parent. When they had children, he'd be there every single day for their kids no matter what happened along the way.

When he got to the studio, Eve didn't have a class in session. Bodey moved to her sleeping quarters and remembered to knock. Every detail seemed crucial to him now. All things must be perfect this time. Rich Kuhl, alias Dickie Burns, answered the door. Behind the man, Bodey could see the old sofa made up as a bed with quilts and a pillow in an embroidered case. The narrow hall was blocked with open suitcases. One of them held women's clothes. A portable easel and paint box sat beside it.

"Eve around? We have some business to discuss." He was determined to keep this unfortunate meeting low key and neutral for his lover's sake.

"My daughter went to drop off her keys at Noreen's house. She's been on the phone all morning telling her students she'll be leaving for an extended vacation. We fly out this afternoon. I can't spend any more time here than necessary," Rich answered Bodey with an oleaginous smile so slick the cowboy wanted to wipe it off his face with a napkin.

"Well, she didn't call me, and I'm one of her students. I need to see her before she makes any rash decisions."

"There's nothing rash about going to live with her long lost father. As I said, I have a palace in the islands compared to this place, and servants to wait on her. My clients are Texans so rich they make your fortune look like tip money. Why I have Arab sheiks and European royalty using my boats. You think a beautiful, talented woman like my Eve won't draw them to her like chum attracts sharks? She can do better than you, cowboy, and I'll see she does."

"Yeah, chum and sharks, that sounds about right. You ever think Eve might be happier right here in Rainbow with a plain, honest man like me? I love your daughter, and I want to marry her. I'd like to have your blessing." Bodey took the ring box from his pocket and showed Dickie Burns the contents.

"That's the best you can do? A semi-precious stone in a silver band. I thought you made some bucks getting stomped on by cows at the rodeo. Easy come, easy go, I guess. It's a good thing Big Ben left you a place to live. No, my princess can do much better, and I've told her so. She needs to give me a chance to make it all up to her."

Determined not to let the man rile him, Bodey put the ring back in his pocket. "The band is platinum, custom made in a pattern that has meaning to us. It's special, like her. Like I said, I need to speak directly to Eve. I'll wait out here."

Bodey took a seat at the small table where he once shared a crowded meal with Evan Adams. He sprawled out his legs and settled in to wait while Rich retreated into the house like a scorpion into its hole. He didn't wait long. Eve drove up fifteen minutes later.

She smiled when she saw Bodey waiting. Taking a seat next to him, she said, "I went by your house, my last stop."

"Why the last stop?"

"Because you are the hardest one to tell. I'm going to spend some time with my father in the islands. He wants to make things right with me. I owe it to him to let him try."

"The way I see it, you don't owe that liar nothing. I could make things right, pay off those bills of yours, and you wouldn't have to leave Rainbow. Be my wife, Eve. Stay with me." The words blundered out again, simple and unadorned, not anything like he'd planned.

Eve turned half away from him. He saw the bruise

he'd given her on her bare upper arm and leaned over to kiss it. She shivered.

"I'm so sorry about that. I'd never hurt you, darlin'. You only got in the way."

"Between you and my father. It could happen again. Look what you did to Evan at the opening. You are far too quick with your fists."

"Sometimes a man must fight for what he wants, but I'd never hit a woman or a child intentionally. I swear." He crossed himself awkwardly hoping that might add weight to his words with Eve.

"Okay, I believe you, but it doesn't matter. Bodey, I've never traveled or seen much of life, and I'm past thirty. As for men, you and Evan were the only ones. I think my father is right to suggest I give him some time before I make any final decisions about my life."

Bodey felt anger rise up and take over his usually amiable disposition. Okay, his words hadn't been eloquent, but they were sincere. She should have understood all she meant to him. Hell, Eve was the only woman he'd ever asked to be his bride. More words, unplanned and hurtful, spewed out.

"So, I'm not a pure enough stud to sire your dozen children. Is that it? I'm a low life bastard, not some A-rab sheik or snotty royal. I'm not good enough for Miss Fancy Pants!"

"Bodey Landrum, I cannot believe you called me that! I thought you knew me better by now. Dozen children, sheiks—are you crazy?"

"I might have landed on my head a few times, but I know you wanted Adams to do the job, and now your daddy wants you for chum!"

"This totally irrational discussion is ended. If I

want to go to visit my dad for a while, I will. Go back to the ranch, cowboy, and castrate some calves, or whatever it is you do when you aren't trying to get into my—fancy pants." Eve stood and stalked back to her house. Standing in her doorway and gloating, Dickie Burns, the triumphant Rich Kuhl, stood sneering at him.

"There are some males I'd like to castrate right now, him, and maybe every slimy sheik and sneaky prince he shoves your way. You want a dozen kids. I can give you a dozen kids," Bodey shouted after her.

"You are incoherent. If you want twelve kids, find someone else. I'm taking a long away-from-you vacation. Live with it!" Eve moved her father aside and closed the door in Bodey's face.

Chapter Seventeen

Bodey went to Mass the next Sunday, and although he mumbled a few prayers for Eve's return, his motives weren't purely religious. After the service, he attached himself to the Niles family, and by persistently following them all the way to their car, wrangled a Sunday dinner invitation.

While Russ oversaw his kids' change of clothes from Sunday best to summer shorts, Bodey loitered in the kitchen getting in Noreen's way as she took a pork roast from the oven and began making the kind of creamed potatoes that came dry in a box. On the back of the range, a lump of frozen green beans gradually thawed in a pot of boiling water.

Bodey leaned on the kitchen counter and watched Noreen whip the dry potato flakes with hot water, milk, and butter.

"I guess no one makes them with real potatoes anymore," he remarked.

"Not if they have two small children and no household help. I make them special by adding a little sour cream. I used to put in chives, too, but the children won't touch them if anything green shows up. Here, make yourself useful."

Noreen handed him a can of refrigerated biscuits. Bodey looked at the container as if she had given him a loaded gun. "For heaven's sake, Bodey, just rap it against the counter and then spread the biscuits out on that cookie sheet. Put the tray in the oven. It's already set."

"I don't do much cookin'. Just have cereal or eggs in the morning, maybe a sandwich for lunch, take my evening meal out. Eve doesn't cook much either. She eats most of her meals at the café or the school cafeteria."

He swung the can of biscuits harder than necessary against the counter's edge. It popped open with a report like a Saturday-night special. As Bodey spread the biscuits, he asked casually, "You heard from Eve? I know you're takin' care of her house."

"There's a postcard from the Cayman Islands on the refrigerator. You didn't get one?" Noreen poked the green beans with a fork to break them up.

"Not yet. She's only been gone a week. Mind if I read yours?"

"Go ahead. While you're over there, pour some milk for the kids. Use the plastic cups."

Bodey turned over the card showing a pristine, palm-studded beach and aqua water. He read the brief message while he poured the milk. "It's beautiful here in the islands. I am painting like mad. Thanks for keeping my plants watered. I'll bring you a nice souvenir. Eve."

"There's no return address." Bodey attached the postcard to the side of the refrigerator again with a magnet shaped like a rooster.

"If you're fishing for her location, she didn't give one. I suspect her daddy doesn't want to advertise his whereabouts. You, me, Russ, and the Sisters are the only ones who know this isn't just a vacation."

With the smack of small sneakers on linoleum flooring, Noreen's children barreled into the kitchen. Little Katie attached herself to her mother's leg. Jesse stuck a finger into the potatoes and licked it off like frosting from a cake.

"Jesse Ted Niles, go set the table the way I showed you. We need an extra place for Uncle Bodey," his mother ordered. "Russ, either take Katie or carve the pork roast, your choice."

Russ picked a carving knife from the rack on the counter and slid the roast on to a wooden board. Bodey, trying to be a good guest, picked up Katie and tickled her tummy until she giggled.

"Don't do that, Bodey. We're toilet-training, and you'll make her wet her pants."

He stopped the tickling immediately. "So you have no clue where Eve is?"

Noreen sighed. "Bodey, if she didn't even send you a postcard, maybe Eve isn't the right woman for you. The two of you certainly aren't soul mates like Russ and I."

"Look, things were going real well between us until her daddy showed up, and how would I know if we were soul mates anyhow? I mean, you married into a family your kin have hated since before the War, and that makes you and Rusty soul mates?" Bodey contended stubbornly.

Behind Noreen, Rusty shook his head and mouthed the words, "Don't go there," as he carved off slices of pork.

"If Eve were your soul mate, you would have known the first time you ever spoke to her, and I understand that didn't go so well when you trapped her on the bridle path."

Bodey glared at his friend who hung his head in mock shame for telling that story about his past.

Noreen went on. "And I do not think if Eve were your soul mate, you would have been on top of Renee in the barn a few hours later. Russ and I just sat in that stall and talked, and we knew. Why, we may even be the reincarnation of the youngest Courville son and the eldest Niles daughter who couldn't marry one hundred seventy-five years ago because, well, they might have been too closely related back then."

"I thought Catholics didn't believe in reincarnation," Bodey countered.

"They don't. I don't. Well, Russ and I finding each other was a miracle that brought our two families together. How about that?" Carrying the bowl of potatoes and a bowl of green beans to the dining room table, Noreen moved past Bodey.

"Whatever you say. I don't see why Eve can't be my miracle. She didn't give you a phone number, did she? Her cell doesn't seem to work outside the country. See, we had a little argument before she left, which might explain why I didn't get a postcard, and I really need to talk to her."

"She said she'd call me if necessary. Give up, Bodey. You and Eve are not compatible, let alone soul mates. Take those biscuits out of the oven before they burn."

She snatched Katie from his arms and took her over to the highchair. Bodey looked down at a large, warm, wet spot on the sleeve of his pale blue dress shirt. Well, he'd rolled in worse stuff. He took the tray of biscuits from the oven, the odor of kiddie urine mingling with the homey smell of baked bread.

"Ah, you might want to check Katie's underwear. She's not wearin' a diaper, I take it."

"No, training pants. Children train better when they can feel the wet."

"That so. I thank you for the dinner invitation, but I think I need to go home and change my shirt. Y'all come over and swim this afternoon. It's hotter than hell outside."

"Hell," repeated Katie softly. Jesse covered his mouth to stifle a laugh.

"Hell," his baby sister repeated at a higher volume, fully savoring the sound.

Bodey patted Katie's soft red curls on his way out the door. "That about says it all, Little Bit."

Chapter Eighteen

Bodey tried the Sisters the following Sunday. He approached them warily as if they could see all the stains on his soul in the bright, hot sun of the churchyard.

"Sorry I didn't take you to lunch last week. I had a dinner invitation from Rusty and his family."

"You aren't obligated to feed us, young man," Sr. Helen assured him.

"With Eve gone, we were surprised—but happy—to see you at Mass," Sr. Inez said.

"So, you heard from Eve? It's been two weeks."

"My, yes. Some lovely postcards. She says she's painting every day and the islands are gorgeous."

"I guess I don't rate a card. Maybe it's payback for the time I went away for two weeks and didn't call because I got so caught up in findin' my daddy. She was the first I told when I returned from Dallas, the only one I wanted to share that with."

"Bodey, we raise young women of character and charity at the Academy—people like Amanda Courville who does so much for the community, and people like Eve who cared enough about Rainbow to help in its revitalization. Our girls are not petty," Sr. Inez asserted.

"Well, there is Renee Hayes," Bodey reminded them as they walked, snail-paced, to his truck.

"You can't win 'em all." Sr. Helen sighed.

"Eve hasn't called me or written or sent an e-mail. I mean, I have my own web site. I'm not that hard to get in touch with, am I?"

"I suspect her father is discouraging contact. After all, if Eve marries a cowboy, she isn't likely to stay with him."

"I'd like to turn that bastard in to the Feds and bring Eve home."

"She'd never forgive you, Bodey. Time and prayer takes care of all things."

Bodey handed their frail old bones into the cab and took the Sisters to Sunday dinner at the café where he noticed a bright postcard of tropical blooms from Eve stuck in the corner of the bar mirror. How much time? How much prayer? A man had only so much patience.

****

Bodey's daddy called at the end of June. A top bull named Black Tuesday was being retired and put out to stud. Patrick O'Shea thought the animal could be purchased for the right price, but he wanted Bodey to come have a looksee. Anything to take his mind off of Eve, Bodey thought, and packed his bags.

"So, what do you think, son?" Pat asked as they observed the black bull, his only white markings around the eyes and muzzle, circling in a paddock.

"Oh, Black Tuesday and me have met before. He still looks in top shape. He was a twister away from my hand as I recall. Never needed to spur Black Tuesday much to get points. That bull needed no encouragement to spin like a tornado. I'd like to try him out again."

"Now that would be sheer foolishness, boy. That beast just retired. You've been out of the ring for over a year."

"They got a chute here?" Bodey asked the ranch manager. "I brought my own bull rope."

While the wranglers dealt with the dangerous business of moving the bull from the paddock to the chute, Pat argued with Bodey. "I don't want you to end up like me—and on some whim, too."

"Look, Dad. I got all this tension in my life right now. I can't think of a better way to forget Eve than eight seconds of sheer terror on the back of a bull. I'm not that out of shape, either."

"Do what you must then, but don't die on me."

Patrick O'Shea in his wheelchair prepared himself to view the ordeal through two slats of fencing. Bodey, bulked up in a borrowed safety vest, pulled on his glove, straddled the chute and adjusted his bull rope, then dropped on to the back of the critter. The chute opened and Black Tuesday charged into the ring, twisting left and bucking high the way Bodey had predicted.

A crowd of ranch hands from wranglers to the cook gathered around the ring and counted off the seconds. Eight of them passed, then ten with Body showing perfect form, sitting straight up, solidly centered, one arm high in the air. At ten seconds, Black Tuesday bunched his massive muscles and shot straight into the air. He came down with a jolt, and Bodey slid one leg over and dismounted, landing on his feet. Patrick let out his breath a moment too soon.

Two-thousand pounds of animal anger bumped Bodey to the ground. For a second, he lay there, not moving. Clyde climbed over the fence and waved a saddle blanket. He hooted and taunted the bull. As Black Tuesday turned his horned head away from the downed man, Bodey rolled to his feet and began backing toward the rail. The bull pawed and charged toward the tiny blanket. Clyde tossed the cloth aside and slid up on the railings. Bodey did the same. Black Tuesday took out his frustration by stomping and tearing the saddle blanket to shreds.

Shaking hands with Clyde for distracting the bull, Bodey made his way back to his father. "Great bull, print out a bill of sale," he remarked.

Pat unclenched his hands from the arms of his wheelchair and spun it to face his son. "There are ways to forget a woman that are easier on my heart, boy."

"But for a good minute there, I didn't think of Eve once. You ever been in love, Pop?" Bodey gave him a dirty-faced grin.

"I fell in love with one of my nurses. Doesn't everyone? A redhead like your mom, one of my weaknesses. But, what did I have to offer her? For all I knew, she'd think I just wanted free nursing care for life. By the time I got my education and a job, she'd married someone else. Eileen Sullivan, that was her name."

"Not so easy to forget, is it?"

"No, but next time try a different remedy."

"Don't tell me time and prayer will accomplish miracles. I've been there, done that, got the T-shirt printed up to wear to church. It ain't working."

"I was going to say hard work, whiskey, and women, but those last two can be almost as risky as bull riding. Take care, son. Take care."

Chapter Nineteen

Eve put the finishing touches on another seascape and turned to the sink to wash away the ultramarine paint of the water and the titanium white of the wave caps from her brushes. Her father's house in the islands proved to be that a little bit of paradise he promised. She could paint four different views from the deck surrounding the building and do close-ups of the brilliant tropical flowers filling the garden.

The staff with their friendly, white smiles and dark faces had to be told not to bother her with offers of mint tea or platters of fresh-cut mangos while she worked. Eve sighed and went outside to flop on to a chaise lounge upholstered in a print of parrots and hibiscus. Immediately, one the servants appeared to ask if she desired to have lunch now. Desire, the only thing she desired was Bodey Landrum. She nodded even though she had no appetite.

Four weeks—and not one word from Bodey. She'd sent him postcards galore—at first, ones describing her dad's house and what she painted, how she relaxed and enjoyed the beach on her first real vacation since she'd finished high school. All were signed with the very corny and trite, "Wish you were here," but she meant it.

So, why didn't he come to find her? The man wasn't stupid. He could track down exactly the kind of livestock he wanted to buy on a computer. True, she couldn't divulge her father's address in case the Feds still looked for him, but every postcard did have a postmark. Once he got to the island, all he had to do was ask for Rich Kuhl's charter boat service. She'd sent him the new e-mail address her father insisted on in case the Feds listened, inserting it in a letter written on borrowed hotel stationery in case he couldn't get away from the ranch to seek her. She'd apologized for their parting argument, though most of it had been his fault, his lack of understanding. He could find a father he never met, who'd done nothing for him, and love him to death, but no, she shouldn't give a man who'd always loved her a second chance.

Eve Burns had her own web site for her art where clients could leave messages for heaven's sake. Why didn't he try that? Perhaps, Bodey still deluded himself with jealousy over foreign princes or had scared himself off with his own strange idea that she wanted to have twelve children. Who knew? They were too different. Their minds didn't work the same.

The maid set the table out on the deck and returned with a tray holding a plate of shrimp salad stuffed in a pineapple half, the fruit neatly cubed for easy eating. The tall, brown woman put down a glass of iced tea and a basket of croissants that instantly reminded Eve of Bodey trying to elbow Evan out of her life during the al fresco lunch on her porch back in Rainbow. A twinge of homesickness made Eve put down her fork with a shrimp halfway to her mouth. She took a long sip of the tea instead to get rid of the lump in her throat.

The commotion of servants that always signaled her father's arrival started by the front door and followed his progress across the house and out onto the deck. His face florid from too much time out on the water, Rich Kuhl took a seat opposite his daughter and ordered the same lunch with the addition of a gin and tonic.

"You certainly are painting up a storm here. I've never seen so many canvases piled up in one place before. The islands must have given you new inspiration," he said.

"Yes, it's wonderful here." Eve did not want to add that without students to teach, tables to wait, and Bodey Landrum to love, she was becoming bored, but her dad must have caught on from the tone of her voice.

"I have a charter this afternoon, an English chap, as they say. Might be a duke or a count or a rock star. Want to come along?"

"No. Last time out on the ocean, I burned pretty badly."

"So, what did you think of Prince Ali? I could see he liked you that day."

"Yes, he did. He said he had no wives or concubines as tall, as fair, or as blonde as me. I believe he was going to approach you about a proper settlement for my sexual services when I informed him that being well over twenty-one and capable of making up my own mind, I had no intention of joining his harem even on a temporary basis."

"Oh, that explains why he cancelled the next day and told me I had to exert better control over my daughter. I can understand why you were upset, but this next guy is a real Englishman, an earl or a software magnate or something. He'll know how you should be treated, Princess."

"Dad, this visit has been great, but I think it's time

I went home."

"Baby, this is your home. You said you would stay all summer at the very least. Believe me, you won't have to wait tables ever again or teach a bunch of rich, little bitches how to paint or ride."

"I was steamed at Bodey when I said I'd stay for three months. He laid this sudden fit of jealousy on me like he couldn't hold his own with any man. The truth is, I miss him and my friends in Rainbow. I've made a place for myself there."

Rich Kuhl sucked up his gin and tonic and gestured for another one. "Didn't you say just yesterday that you hadn't heard from the cowboy? My guess is he has already moved on to someone else. Men like him don't go without sex for more than a week. If he cared, why isn't he here?"

"He has a ranch to run, a business to set up."

"If he loved you half as much as I do, he'd come for you."

"I've written him again—on the hotel stationery like you asked so no one would figure out our real location. If he should show up at the resort, they will tell him where to find me. Mail it for me on your way out, will you?"

"Anything my princess wants." Rich Kuhl dug into his shrimp salad with gusto.

Chapter Twenty

Bodey tried the work cure first. He saw to his own stock, worked with Fancy who only reminded him of Eve, and helped Rusty around his place. Being worn out guaranteed a good night's sleep until dawn, when he woke from dreams of Eve mounted over him and a woody that wouldn't go away until he hit the cold shower. He supposed he should take down the two pictures of her—his primitive version and Evan's detailed masterpiece flanking his bedroom door—but that would be admitting weakness. The paintings were fine art, nothing more, even if his decorator said they didn't go well with the southwest color scheme of adobe with turquoise accents.

Two weeks before the Academy was due to resume classes, the Sisters said they hadn't heard if Eve planned to teach art and riding again the coming semester. When he took them to the Sunday buffet, he noticed the bar mirror at the Rainbow Café festooned with postcards from the islands received by all the staff from Ja'nae to the busboy. Bodey felt particularly low every time he went in the place.

All that Mass going and praying with no results got him down, too. The Sisters had started introducing him to other Academy old girls, unmarried ones, and that was the most depressing part of all. If the nuns had given up on Eve's return, why shouldn't he?

The private detective he'd hired by phone on the island where all the cards were postmarked, so far had come up with nothing about Eve. Rich's charters picked up passengers, went out to sea, and returned to the docks. No sign of a tall blonde woman with them. On his own, he'd found a web site for Kuhl's Deep Sea Charters and sent message after message to Eve in the contact box. Once, he'd made up an assumed name—Lord Godfrey Blackham—and tried to charter a boat simply to get directions to the business, but Rich Kuhl was no fool. His clients were picked up at the airport by the captain, himself, and whisked away to deep sea adventure off the coast of a privately owned secret island, or so said the advertising blurb. One look at Bodey and the captain would be certain his guest went overboard while out at sea.

He considered dressing up like an Arab sheik, but didn't think he could pull off the disguise with his Texas accent. What if he did discover the island holding Eve, and she didn't want him? There he'd be clothed in one of those long, white dresses with a rag on his head and sandals on his feet. She'd laugh her head off. Even a poor, bastard cowboy like himself had more pride than to do that.

Or did he? Going to the islands seemed like the only way to find and confront Eve, tell her how he truly felt. He'd need help. Only one man he could trust in any situation. He called Rusty and invited himself over with a six-pack of beer and a large, greasy bag of Mama Tyne's pork cracklings. Unfortunately, Noreen had put the kids to bed and settled in right beside her husband. She began to laugh almost immediately as he laid out his plans.

"You, Bodey, with that Texas drawl, trying to pass as an Arab? And those blue eyes, how are you going to explain those?" She laughed so hard the beer she purloined came out her nose, and she had to stop long enough to wipe it.

"I tell you I've thought it all out. I can get brown contacts easy, and I'll wear shades the whole time. I'm tan enough now, I think, but I can lay out by the pool to get darker. My hair is black. I'll let my beard grown in and cover the cleft in my chin. We'll just say I don't speak much English and Rusty is my interpreter."

"Oh no, you don't, Bodey Landrum. You will not draw my husband into this. What if Rich Kuhl has armed guards? He seems paranoid enough for that."

Bodey considered for a minute. "Nope, he runs a charter fishing service. He isn't running drugs or anything. At least, I hope not for Eve's sake. Might have his own gun, but I can carry one, too. Those robes would make concealment pretty easy."

"You can't take one on an airplane."

"So I'll get a weapon there. Look Noreen, this is between Russ and me. You got no say."

Rusty finished crunching a crackling. He took a slow, deliberate swig of beer before he spoke. "Shows how little you know about women and marriage. Why don't you go in the kitchen for a minute, Bodey, and let me talk to my wife."

Bodey went, but he didn't go far. He lingered by the door listening. He knew what hand the man held, what card Rusty would play to win against Noreen's objections.

"Noreen, my soul mate, Bodey isn't as lucky as us. He didn't recognize the woman he loved right from the start like I did, and maybe I got in the way of that. You remember I told you how Eve scorned him on the bridle path the day of this eighteenth birthday? He intended to try again, but I called Renee to come to the party because I couldn't afford a birthday gift for my best friend."

Noreen nodded, a little misty-eyed. "Yes, if you hadn't made that call, we might not have met at all, but I still believe we would have since we were fated to be together."

"Right, it worked for us, but it's like I put Renee in his path to true love like ours. I made him swerve away from Eve."

"Don't you take the blame for that, Rusty Niles! If Bodey had dated Eve instead, he would have taken advantage of her innocence and then left her to follow the rodeo trail. The life he's led, the women he's had, he doesn't deserve Eve. She's still very naïve, and he went and seduced her the moment he got into town."

Rusty took a deep breath and another sip of beer. "Darling, from what Bodey tells me, Eve knew exactly what to do in bed."

"The two of you discussed her as if she were some cheap stripper—or Renee?"

"Not in detail, only in general. He needs another chance with Eve. I owe him that. He means to marry her. I've seen the ring."

"So you go off on this escapade and leave me here with two small children." Noreen pouted and consoled herself with a crackling—like dining on bacon only better.

"I promise you I'll save all I can and take you to the islands for a vacation one day."

"Oh, Russ, we can't afford that. I'm worried something bad will happen to you."

Rusty took Noreen into his arms, held her tight. "I won't let anything go wrong, and if it does, you know we'll meet in another lifetime."

"Can I come back now?" Bodey shouted from the kitchen. "We have to nail down the details of the trip." He didn't wait for an answer, but sauntered out and picked up his beer again.

"Looks like we're going to the Cayman Islands with Noreen's blessing." Rusty clinked his bottle against Bodey's.

"Hardly. If anything bad happens to Rusty, I will never forgive you, Bodey Landrum. I'm going to bed. Make what plans you will. And take those cracklings with you when you leave. They go straight to my hips."

Noreen marched down the hallway. Bodey figured she would have slammed the door if the kids weren't sleeping.

"Good. I'll make reservations with Rich Kuhl under the name Omar Abu Something-or-other, a rich as Croesus oil well-owning Arab. I already found a place online where I can get authentic clothing. Give me a week or so to let my beard grow out and see about the contacts. We can use the time to decide what you should wear and how we'll communicate. If this succeeds, I'll bankroll that trip to the Caribbean for you and Noreen."

****

Bodey had to say the cotton robes provided a certain airy comfort in the heat and humidity of the islands. His headpiece kept the sun off his neck and his feet stayed nice and cool in the heavy sandals. He'd changed into his disguise stowed in his carry-on luggage in the airport restroom after passing through security. Up till then, he'd still been blue-eyed Bodey Landrum according to his passport—with the addition of a short beard. Though he hadn't sweated through the armpits yet, Rusty looked damned uncomfortable in the wrinkled white linen suit, pink shirt, and Panama hat he'd worn for the whole trip.

Russ ran a finger around his uncomfortable collar. He rarely wore a dress shirt except for a few hours on Sunday. "You sure Rich won't recognize me?"

"I don't think Rich is the kind of guy who notices underlings, especially kids who parked his car fifteen years ago. You've grown up, filled out, and got a nice, manly stubble now to cover some of those freckles."

"Yeah, it's hot and itchy and Noreen hates the beards, yours and mine both." Rusty scrubbed his hands over the reddish bristles on his cheeks.

"Well, you only started yours last week. It feels better when it grows out." Bodey fingered the end of his black beard, close-cut but coming to a point at the bottom of his chin. He hated poking the brown contacts into his eyes. The things you did for women or true love as Rusty might say. "Hush now, here he comes."

The charter boat chugged to the dock. Two brawny black men threw out the lines and secured it to the pilings. Rich Kuhl, captain's hat at a cocky angle on his white hair, jumped ashore with a mouthful of apologies. "Sorry to be late, Prince Omar. I'll reimburse you for that cab. Usually, I meet my clients at the airport, but we had a little engine trouble. She's working fine now."

"Please speak more slowly. The prince has little English, but understands some. I am his translator,

Aaron Marchand." Noreen had helped him pluck the name from their mutual ancestors, but Bodey teased Rusty about it sounding kind of gay. No more so than the white suit and pink shirt Roger lent him, but he added, "I picked up Arabic when I served in Operation Desert Storm, marine corps" to make sure Rich knew he served as some kind of bodyguard, too.

"Sorry-I-am-late. We-go-now-to-eat-a-good-meal-on-my-private-island-then-fish." Rich spoke slowly and very loud as if volume would break down the communication gap. He ended with a salaam-like flourish straight out of the *Arabian Night*s.

Rusty whispered in Bodey's ear. The Arab prince nodded graciously.

"The wind is picking up. Maybe you should stow the prince in the cabin, Mr. Marchand. Help yourselves to anything in cooler. I need to take the helm. The boys will get your bags."

Getting tangled in his robes a little, Bodey descended less than gracefully into the boat followed by his minion. They made themselves comfortable in leather captain's chairs and raided the cooler for bottles of cold water.

Left alone, Bodey ventured, "Great, we're going straight to Eve. Now, we won't have to mess around pretendin' to fish. I can chuck this disguise and have my heart-to-heart with her, then the three of us will head back to the states." If his blue eyes hadn't been covered by muddy brown contacts and wrap-around sunglasses, they would have glittered.

"Too easy, way too easy. Something is bound to go wrong." The sound of the boat engine covered their conversation. Rusty unbuttoned his collar and stripped off a white silk tie, also courtesy of Roger. The hell with it. What he did for Bodey Landrum!

They were on the water quite a while before a small island peeked from the sea. Entering a cove sheltered from the wind that had made the trip rough, the boat, another *Princess Eve,* docked again. Rich came to the side of his wealthy passenger and directed them up a path where tropical plants crowded the way.

"Like Eden," Bodey murmured to Rusty. Where else would Eve live?

A feast of coconut shrimp, rice pilaf, tropical fruits, and a bowl of hummus surrounded by pita strips to make the customer feel at home awaited them. A hyacinth macaw begged for grapes from a nearby perch. Iced tea sat on the table, but Rich offered chilled champagne. When Bodey held out a hand, Rusty kicked him in the shin under the table. He slammed it on the chair arm instead.

"You have offended the prince. He adheres strictly to the laws of Islam," Rusty explained.

"Well, it's been my observation that some of them play hooky when on vacation and imbibe a bit. Anything else I can get for him?"

Bodey gestured Rusty to come close and whispered in his ear. "Tell him I like women, white women." So far the only females he'd seen ran to the dusky side.

"Since we are staying the night, he wonders if you might have any white women available."

A deep frown creased Rich's florid face. "Only my daughter and she's not here right now."

More whispers. "The prince wants only the pleasure of her company. He would treat her with the greatest respect."

"Maybe she'll come to dinner. Maria, when you see my daughter, explain the prince wants to meet her tonight," he said to the woman bringing a tray of light desserts. "Finish up. Looks like a storm is brewing on the horizon. We might be able to get in some fishing before it hits."

Bodey gestured to his translator and whispered, "Doesn't sound safe."

Rusty answered back, "You booked a fishing service, not me." At full voice, he said, "I'd like to change. The prince will remain dressed as he is."

"Certainly. Your room is right over there."

Rusty eased by the parrot with the impressive beak breaking Brazil nuts and jostled his stand. The blue wings flapped, and the bird squawked, "Pretty Eve, Pretty Eve," for no reason at all, but it seemed to taunt Bodey with its harsh voice and beady eyes.

"Excuse, please," Bodey managed, trying hard to sound foreign. Giving the parrot a wide berth, he followed Rusty.

In the privacy of the bathroom, he heaved up his robes and took a leak. Going commando under his costume sure came in handy in a hurry. He'd been holding it for some time. Rusty changed into khaki shorts, a polo shirt, and his own sandals. "I don't care if translators wear suits, I'm not going fishing in one," he complained.

Bodey ignored the complaint. "We're close. That parrot knows her."

"Her daddy probably trained it to peck out the eyes of any man who comes near his daughter. You see the beak on that bird?"

"Yeah, but if I can handle a two-ton bull, I can deal

with a parrot. Not so sure about the fishing expedition. Almost puked just getting here."

"Your idea," Russ reminded him again.

They rejoined Rich and his crew, cast off, and headed out to sea searching for marlin. Instead, they caught two large yellowfin tuna after copious compliments to the sheik on his upper body strength and endurance.

"You tell the prince we'll grill these for his dinner and get him a marlin tomorrow for sure," Rich said to Rusty. "We need to go in now, race that storm coming at us. Tell him my beautiful daughter will be waiting. He's looking a little green and that should encourage him to hang in there until we get back to the island."

The ship turned and began to buck through swell after swell. They swerved again to run along the calmer water of the main island, but by that time Bodey, doubled over, hugged the railing and puked over the side. The captain turned the wheel over to one of his men and came to show his concern for his very rich passenger with several strong pats on the back. Bodey's sunglasses fell into the sea. One contact popped out and joined them. He had enough presence of mind to shut his eye pretending he'd gotten salt water in it and gestured for Rich to go away, but another turn of the boat caused the wind to swell under his authentic Arabic throbe. It carried the cloth up and over his bare buttocks as he hunched heaving into the sea. He'd spent days by his pool tanning his feet and legs for this adventure, but sure, he'd worn trunks never thinking Rich Kuhl would get a look-see at his lily-white ass.

He knew the gig was up when Kuhl's big hands seized his shoulders and spun him around. "You're no

Arab." He forced Bodey's closed eye open and stared into the shining blue iris. "You're that no good cowboy sniffing around my daughter again. She's not interested in lowering herself for a guy like you. Now get off my boat!"

Get off the boat! They were on the ocean. Oh sure, Bodey could see the beach from here, but he still reckoned it to be a mighty long swim. He backed toward the center of the craft where he could make a better stand as Rich summoned the spare deckhand, a big man black as sin and twice as strong. Though Rusty tried to yank the muscleman off, he ended up sitting on his own ass on the deck. With the deckhand gripping him around the torso and Rich pushing from behind, Bodey went over the side. "Swim for it, you bastard!" Kuhl shouted as Bodey, weakened by sea sickness, surfaced.

"As for you, Aaron Marchand, or whoever you are, I figure he hired you for this escapade. I'll take you back to the dock. Get yourself on a plane and get out of here."

In the water, Bodey struggled, the robe wrapping around his legs. Spending every summer doing rodeo, he hadn't made good use of Big Ben's pool and now lived to regret it. His arms were plenty strong enough, but his swimming skills lacked a great deal. He turned to float on his back, but the garment still dragged him down. He ripped off the headdress and freed his head to ride a little higher in the water. One desperate blue eye watched Rusty shuck off his sandals and do a pretty decent dive into the surf. He moved toward Bodey with an even stroke. That was Rusty, steady, dependable. He didn't deserve his friendship anymore than he did a woman like Eve, strange thoughts as he swallowed a gulp of seawater and realized he was going under.

A hand jerked him to the surface again and towed him with an arm wrapped around his bearded chin toward the combers that raked a sandy beach. They rode the waves in and emerged from the water to sprawl just above the waterline. Rusty pressed his back frantically to bring up the saltwater. What was a little more barfing after what he'd just experienced?

"Enough! I didn't swallow that much. You got to me real quick. Besides, I'm mostly empty from all that hurling." Bodey rolled over and sat up beside his best friend. "Sorry I got you into this, sorry I lost Eve, sorry I didn't put out money for the izaar."

"The what?"

"The thing you wear under your throbe to cover your ass. You sure covered mine just now, but can we *not* tell Noreen?"

"She won't hear it from me, or I'll never get out of the house alone again."

"Still got your passport and credit card? The danged pouch almost strangled me in the waves." Bodey fished out a zippered plastic bag on a long string from the neck of his sodden robe and Rusty did the same. People who'd seen them struggle from the sea gathered, forming a ring around them, offering to call for aid.

"We're fine. Just point us in the direction of a place where we can buy some dry clothes. And no, we didn't have a great time in the Cayman Islands if anyone wants to know," Bodey said, his voice raw from seawater and vomit.

The rain began to patter and pockmark the sand.

Well-meaning arms helped them up, mouths offered them water and a ride into town.

"Come on, Rusty. Let's go home."

****

At the house, Eve sat on one of the lounges watching the rain pour from the eaves as it did fairly often this time of day. She'd been thinking about Bodey, about going home, but did not share her thoughts with her father who would only find reasons for her to stay.

"How was the fishing?" she asked to show interest in his life.

"No marlin. Two nice yellowfins we can cut into steaks for dinner."

"Where are your guests?"

"Turned out that Arab had no stomach for the sea. He puked his guts out and begged me to put him ashore on Grand Cayman so he could go back to his oil rich desert. What a wuss, but I get to keep his money."

One of the crewmen walked by with the prince's luxurious leather suitcase. Eve raised her eyebrows. "Don't you fret, honey, we'll get it back to the man tomorrow. Glad you came out of hiding to have dinner with me."

"I love having dinner with you, Daddy, making up for all those lost years. Sorry I hid out at lunchtime, but I simply couldn't stomach another sheik leering at me throughout a meal. I saw the man dressed in a throbe get off the boat and headed for the hills to do some sketches, but I did intend to meet you at dinner. I know it helps your business to have a hostess."

"That's why I'd like you to stay here. You are good for business, good for me, too. Like I said, this Bodey

217

character must have moved on or he'd have tried to reach you by how."

"Regardless, I have to go back to Rainbow soon and close up my studio, let the Academy know my plans if I don't intend to teach art and riding this fall. I might do a short retreat and sort out my feelings."

"Your daddy understands. You do that, then hurry back to me. I'll keep my eye out for a rich man who deserves you."

Chapter Twenty-One

Yep, the time had come for the whiskey cure after the disguise debacle. Maybe he'd pick up some honky-tonk gal to fill the hole Eve had left, but hell, it would take a hundred loose women just to cover the bottom of that pit, let alone top it off. Still, he wasn't ready for the nice ladies the nuns were pushing his way. He wanted to settle down, and maybe once Eve was out of his system, he'd try again.

The Rainbow Express boiled on an August Saturday night. The rickety air conditioning system couldn't cope with the ninety-three degree evening outside or the crush of bodies inside. Sweat ran down the necks of women and tantalized by disappearing into their cleavage like warm streams flowing over boulders.

A good zydeco band played and between drinks, Bodey danced with girls who had so many piercings he knew they were too young for him and older gals smelling of cigarettes and gin, who looked like they'd given up on every other pleasure in life. He hadn't bothered to shave since returning to Rainbow. The women told him the pointed beard made him look devilish and they hoped he'd live up to it, but he didn't favor any one of them.

About the time he started tripping over his own feet, he gave his truck keys to a bartender who couldn't be much past twenty-one, and pointing out his vehicle, asked the kid to see he got home to Three B's Ranch just down the road. He'd promised his daddy he would be careful if he drank. It was good to have someone who cared about him.

The bartender slung the keys beneath the counter and rolling his eyes said, "I guess, whatever." When Bodey pulled out three hundred dollars to pay his tab, the remainder to serve as a tip, the answer changed to, "Yessir."

By the time last call came and the crowd had thinned down to the die-hards and the drunks, Bodey sat with his head resting on the bar. He wasn't sleeping or passed out, only trying to figure out how to get to his truck without puking. A hot body took possession of the stool next to him and slid the seat closer so their elbows touched. Bodey raised his head enough to see over his arms. He focused. "Renee?"

"You need a ride home, cowboy?"

"Soon," said Bodey, swallowing hard.

"Looks like both of us were screwed over by artists. You know that snake, Evan, must have painted me fifty times, mostly in the nude, had a big showing and wouldn't cut me in on the profits. Said I'd signed the modeling contract and been given cash plus room and board in San Francisco—and then he mocked my art."

"Mocking's bad," Bodey agreed.

"So, did Eve take the check Hardy gave her for her mural and any other services she might have rendered him and skip to the islands, or did she hit you for the cash to set up elsewhere?"

"Daddy came," Bodey explained as best as he could.

"She got herself another sugar daddy? Pure, pious Eve? Where does she find people like that in Rainbow? Wish I knew. There's one thing I do know. Revenge is sweet. How about we take some revenge on artists, Bodey?"

"Swheet revenge," he parroted.

"Where are your keys?" Renee began searching his pants pockets as well as exploring other possibilities along the way.

"Here they are, ma'am," the boy bartender offered. The drunk wouldn't remember who drove him home come morning.

Renee wrinkled her nose at being called ma'am, but took the keys. "Thanks—sonny."

She maneuvered Bodey across the gravel lot to the passenger door of his truck. "You can drive schtick?" he asked.

"All my life."

Bodey motioned her to go around to the driver's seat. Renee started the engine. The noise drowned the retching sound of Bodey puking his guts out behind the right front tire. Finally, wiping his lips on his sleeve, he crawled in beside her.

The last of the evening didn't go much smoother back at the ranch. By the time Renee got Bodey to his bed—thank heaven the master suite was on the first floor—and pulled off his boots and jeans, the cowboy king started snoring. Oh well, no problem. She'd get naked and slip in beside him. In the morning, he'd believe anything and Eve Burns would be just a bitter memory to both of them.

Renee shimmied out of her red spandex dress and let it puddle at the foot of the bed. She hung her crimson lace thong over Evan's painting of *Venus Rising from her Bath*. Renee snorted. Evan had done one of her in a similar pose and given it the same title. She was definitely the better Venus, far more voluptuous. She pitched her ice pick heels to opposite corners of the room and snuggled up to Bodey like a rattlesnake against a hot rock on a cold evening.

****

The sun had been up for hours by the time Renee opened her eyes and pushed away from Bodey who still snored with a sound like the evening freight train. She stretched, admiring her body in the bedroom mirror. Taking a closer look, Renee smoothed out the make-up that had sunken into the fine lines around her eyes with her fingertips. She should shower, but she had left all of her cosmetics at home.

A brief skinny dip, head above water, should do the trick. Afterward, she could work on a full body tan. Seeing her completely naked out by the pool would give old Bodey a jolt when he finally came to. Renee snatched a thick, over-sized towel from Bodey's bathroom and, admiring the artistic strewing of her clothing from last night, started across the room. She had a second thought.

She checked both night tables and found what she wanted in the one closest to Bodey's side of the bed. Tearing the packet open and tossing it aside, she inserted her two longest fingers in the condom and stretched it. Then, pulling it off, she spit into the opening, rubbed the contents around, and draped the forged evidence over one of the small turquoise-colored pots the decorator had used to bring the room together. Something glittered in the bottom of the little container.

Renee drew out a ring with a stone of gorgeous purple amethyst in its center. The setting definitely had the sheen of platinum and the look of hand wrought art. It went well with her current shade of auburn hair. She slipped the ring over her knuckle. Loose, made for a bigger hand, but definitely not something Bodey would wear. Maybe, another woman had left it here. Or the ring had been intended for another woman. Perhaps, Bodey would take the hint and give it to her once he saw her wearing nothing but the ring. Smiling a big, toothy grin, Renee went for her swim.

In San Francisco, she had been cold all the time, partly because she posed in the nude for a great deal of her sojourn, but also because the evening fogs rolled in chilling her bones and the winds whipped off the cold waters of the bay. Here, in August the pool water fairly steamed, and the sun gave off brutal rays at eleven a.m. Renee took a short dip to get rid of the bar smell, then greasing herself with a found tube of lotion, she spread the thick towel over the lounger and did some full frontal sunbathing with only her face covered by a corner of the bath sheet. Must watch out for future wrinkles, but men did so love seeing her tanned all over. The thought of how she got that way turned them on, especially when she revealed no sprays or machines were involved, simply spreading herself in the great outdoors.

About the time Renee felt she should turn over or burn, the doorbell rang. She could wrap up and get that for Bodey, but truly, she'd rather have the man to herself today. He owed her at least one favor, and she intended to collect. She rolled over onto her stomach and stretched out like a lazy cat. Indoors, she could hear

Bodey blundering around, then stomping across his great room toward the door.

"Dammit, who's layin' on that bell? Jesus, who opened those drapes? I haven't done anything this damned stupid since I turned twenty-four."

Pausing at the door, Bodey seized a battered, black cowboy hat from a rack and pulled it low over his eyes to protect himself from the onslaught of sunshine. He tugged at the zipper of his half-closed jeans, but it remained jammed.

"What the hell do you want!" he shouted as he flung open the heavy door and flinched from the light and the sight of Eve Burns with her finger on the bell.

"Oh, God help me."

"I'm back. I tried to call you last night from the Dallas terminal. It doesn't matter. Noreen brought my car to the airport in Lafayette. I came here as soon as I dropped her off. I need to know why you never answered my letters," she said quietly.

"Letters?" Bodey answered, rubbing his furry chin.

Judging by the way it felt, he had puke caught in the hairs, and since the light hurt his eyes and made him squint, he must look awful. Yep, his breath did smell like vomit and whiskey. What a fine way to greet the woman he loved.

Then, something even worse happened. A feminine arm snaked across his shoulder and draped over his bicep. The hand wore Eve's engagement ring. He turned his head and looked into the predatory green eyes of Renee Hayes. She wore nothing but the ring and a bath towel casually knotted over one full breast.

"Shit," he said.

"Never mind. I have my answer. You chose Renee

again." Eve backed up a step.

"Don't go, Eve. I want you to see the beautiful ring Bodey gave me last night." Renee held out her hand. Eve backed up another step as if trying to escape a rattler ready to strike.

Bodey seized Renee's wrist and jerked the ring from her finger. "I might have been drunker than a Baptist on a binge last night, but I never gave you this ring. It's Eve's ring."

He held it out in his palm. The bright light shot off the metal and went right to the back of his brain. "The ring that wasn't good enough for Princess Eve from the man who wasn't good enough for her either."

"I don't know where you got that idea."

"I think I'm gonna be sick." Bodey turned tail and ran for the bathroom. Eve followed him. Renee strolled along after them. She'd let Eve get a good look at the bedroom first, the covers tossed on both sides of the bed, the thong draped across Eve's picture, the used condom. Eve was an artist. She'd take in all the details.

Renee waited until the barfing stopped, the toilet flushed, and the water stopped running. When she slunk into the bedroom, Bodey was stretched out on the covers, his head propped up with pillows and cold, wet washcloths plastered across his eyes and throat.

"Can't decide which is worse, this or seasickness."

Eve didn't respond to the odd remark. She touched the back of his hand. "Take care, Bodey. Here's Renee. I wish you every happiness." She stood and left the room.

Renee sank down in the spot vacated by Eve. Bodey peeled off the washcloth covering his eyes. "Oh, it's you again."

"That's the thanks I get for driving you home and taking care of all your wants and needs last night, Bodey Landrum," Renee simpered. "You should beg me to take that ring."

"The bartender was supposed to drive me. I sure did pay him enough to do the job. Leave the ring alone, get dressed, and go on home, Renee. Given a choice, I'd rather die alone."

Chapter Twenty-Two

"Dad, I tried work, and outside of gettin' a lot done, I still saw Eve's face every time I closed my eyes. So, I moved on to whiskey the other night, and evidently tried another woman, but I can't remember much about that. I also did a crazy stunt that I'm just too embarrassed to tell you about right now."

Despite his misery, Bodey couldn't help but appreciate how good it felt to have a father listening on the other end of the line.

"How'd all that go for you, son?"

"Poorly. Haven't had a drunk like that in a good ten years. Forgot how bad you feel in the morning. Then, I found a nekkid woman in my swimmin' pool. Considering all the evidence, we had a mighty good time, but I don't remember a minute of it."

"Bodey, boy, I told you to be careful."

"I paid the bartender to drive me home, but it seems Renee took over at the club. That's not the worst part. Eve came back."

"She caught you with the nekkid lady, right?"

"That's right."

"Sorry I even suggested those other remedies. Is there any hope you and Eve will get back together?"

"It's not lookin' good. She won't answer her phone or come to the door. I fear she might have gone back to her daddy. No sign of life around her place. It's all closed up."

"How about those nuns she's so tight with? Do they know where she is? Would they talk reason with her?"

"I don't know, Pop. I'm going over to the convent as soon as we hang up here."

"Good luck, son. I'd sure like to have some pretty grandchildren. *Vaya con Dios.*"

****

Bodey shuffled his feet in front of the reception desk while a stern-faced, middle-aged nun looked him up and down. "Sr. Helen is resting right now and unavailable. You might find Sr. Inez in the stables. I believe she is overseeing the cleaning there," the Sister finally divulged. "You will need a pass to go there. Please don't wander the grounds as it is not visiting day."

The nun wrote on a slip of paper and without a smile, handed it to Bodey. He'd gone to public school, but now figured he knew how kids who attended parochial schools felt—guilty, whether they were or not.

"Thank you, ma'am, I mean, Sister."

Bodey jammed the hat he had been crushing in his hands back on to his head and headed for the stables. From a distance, he could see Sr. Nessy leaning heavily on her cane, silhouetted in the central doorway of the barn. Her voice reached him from afar.

"Put your back into it! When I was twice your age, I could muck out the whole place myself in half a day."

The two novices who had volunteered for the job as an act of charity looked at each other across the wheelbarrow and continued methodically forking up manure and soiled straw in a rather dainty manner. They were racking up points in Heaven for sure.

"Bodey Landrum! Did you come to help or to grovel?" Sr. Inez snapped as soon as she caught sight of him.

"Both, Sister. Why, I've won buckles for my work with a pitchfork," he drawled, hoping to get on her good side.

"I don't doubt that, but there is no need to brag. We missed you at Mass this Sunday." Sr. Nessy didn't smile when she said it.

"I was, ah—indisposed." Bodey took the pitchfork from a relieved novice. He laid in with a will despite the clean, pressed clothes and shiny new boots he had put on to visit the convent. Sweat dribbled down his clean-shaved face. When visiting a convent, not a good idea to resemble the Devil.

"So we've heard."

"Already?" Bodey grimaced. "How about if you let these little ladies go back to their prayers, and I'll finish up here."

The second novice gave him a grateful smile and propped her pitchfork against a wall. "Sister, with your permission," she hopefully asked Nessy.

"Go. Your help was most welcome." As the novices rushed off in un-nun like haste, she muttered, "City girls."

Bodey got into the corners of the last two stalls, filled the wheelbarrow, and dumped the load on to the manure pile. He man-handled a bale of straw closer to the doors, cut the binding with his pocket knife, and forked up clean bedding.

"Good job," Sr. Inez conceded. "I don't suppose

this is an act of contrition?"

"Shoveling sh—manure? No, ma'am. I do it every day, at least lately."

"So, you're really here to discuss Eve. You made our girl cry, Bodey Landrum, when she held up dry-eyed all during her father's disappearance and her mother's illness. Don't expect to get off easy."

"No, ma'am. I'll do anything you say if I can get a chance to talk to Eve again. I know things looked bad over at my place, but you see, I have no memory of havin' fuc—ah, sinned with Renee Hayes. She just showed up. I had a lot to drink the night before, and—"

"That is no excuse," Sr. Inez said sternly.

"A piss-poor one at best, I agree, but Eve is the only woman I want. She's the woman I love. I waited nearly three months for any word or sign from her, went to the islands to track her down and that didn't go so good. It all wore me down and I turned to the bottle just the one time, but still I don't feel guilty like I should if I'd really done something."

"We told you time and prayer would take care of you and Eve. To God and the universe, three months is a snap of the fingers, fast work at that. Had you waited one more day, this mess would not have happened," Sr. Inez scolded.

Bodey, leaning on the pitchfork, his head bowed, answered, "Yes, ma'am."

"What would you do now if Eve gave you another chance?"

"Why, I'd take Eve up on my horse and ride off into the sunset with her. We'd live happily ever after, I swear to God." He looked into the nun's stern eyes to show he meant it. She appeared to be gauging his sincerity and overall worth.

"Not much of a plan, Bodey Landrum, but God and I will see what we can do. Meet me here at eight this evening. Better keep that pass or Sr. Carola will have your balls on a platter for breakfast.

Bodey's black eyebrows shot up at her language, but he answered, "Yes, ma'am, Sister."

****

Lying on her cot in the small retreat cottage, Eve considered getting up and having her bread and water for dinner. She fasted to purge her body of three months of easy living in the islands and her love of Bodey Landrum. Perhaps, if she had been able to untangle herself from her father sooner, Renee Hayes would not have taken Bodey from her again. On the other hand, who knew when he'd started sleeping with Renee— maybe the day after she'd gone off with her dad?

She merely tormented herself thinking about it when she should be contemplating entering the convent again. Maybe that used condom draped over the turquoise bowl had been a sign from God that Eve Burns did not belong in the real world. Could be she'd fasted too much because dreams arrived featuring a stern, gray-eyed nun she recognized as the Academy's founder, Mother Leontine. The Lady Mother pointed a long, strong finger as large as a man's at Eve and proclaimed, "You cannot hide from life in the convent. I will not permit this to happen. Go to the man who loves you." The apparition appeared to float above the floor of the cabin. Reputed to be six-feet tall and large-boned according to legend, Mother Leontine retained a commanding presence even as a ghost, an incorporeal woman not to be defied.

Had all that wild, crazy sex with Bodey taken away her option to enter the order? No, God would forgive her if she asked, and He trumped Mother Leontine, no matter how intimidating, any day. Still, had she experienced a vision, or did she merely use the dream to reinforce her true desire to return to Bodey?

Eve turned to contemplative exercise. It did not help. Numerous walks on the long, crooked path to the statue of the Magdalene failed to aid her in reaching a decision. She kept staring at the path, waiting for Bodey to appear on his paint horse and carry her away. No, that door had closed, and the Lord would open a window as He had for the novice, Maria, in *The Sound of Music*. Oh right, Maria had married the man, not taken her final vows. Think of another window, Eve, think of anything but Bodey Landrum. Too depressed to get up, Eve drifted off to sleep, her dreams as impure as her prior thoughts.

She and Bodey lay in the wisteria glade again. They were both naked, a true Adam and Eve appreciating the best free thing God had put on earth. She went on all fours and Bodey mounted her like a stallion, pulling back her head by her long, pale hair, making her look up and right into the eyes of Sr. Helen. Eve rolled to her feet so suddenly she miscalculated and hit the floor with a crash.

"Are you in there, child?" Sr. Helen's quavery voice called. "Did you pass out from fasting? That happens. Don't be embarrassed. Please let me in."

Eve got up, straightened her wrinkled white blouse, and pulled down the beige riding pants that had bunched up between her legs during her nap. She patted her hair, and found that despite her dream, it remained tightly braided down her back and secured with the little black bow.

"Coming, Sr. Helen. I'm fine, only a little dizzy."

"You must eat and drink. Here, sit down and have your bread and water. I'd like you to go for a walk with me, and you will need your strength."

"I don't really feel like walking, Sr. Helen. I've been to the shrine a half dozen times and have felt no relief, gotten no answers."

"Oh, but the evening is lovely, and one never knows when God or one of his saints will answer a prayer. Finish that roll and wash your face with a little cold water. Put on your boots. Then, we shall venture out in search of a miracle.

****

Wearing fresh clothes and smelling of aftershave, Bodey showed up right on time. Sr. Inez handed him the reins of a horse that seemed to have a bit of a weight problem. His big belly dwarfed the already small, hornless English saddle. She introduced them.

"This is Brownie. He's a nice Anglo-Arab who likes his feed and won't gallop without some urging. We put the smallest children on him because he is so sluggish. Still, he's a good boy, and the only mount I have trained to come at a whistle. Unfortunately, he was taught to come for treats by his former owner."

"So, we're takin' an overweight horse for a walk? Where does Eve come in on this?" Bodey asked as he led the horse out of the barn and followed Sr. Inez down a path covered in pine needles.

"If Eve gives you a second chance and you want to ride off into the sunset with her, all you have to do is whistle for Brownie."

****

Eve held Sr. Helen's gently trembling arm as they strolled along the pine needle path. "You're right. It is a beautiful evening, soothing to the soul—now that the sun is going down. The day was scorching earlier."

"Exactly. The atmosphere has cooled. It's time to reconsider."

"Reconsider what?" Eve asked as they came to the clearing holding the shrine to the Magdalene.

Her heart clenched as she let her eyes stray toward the path where Bodey had once appeared riding his paint horse to scoop her up and carry her into the tangle of wisteria, into their tangled relationship. A racket on the opposite path broke in on her romantic memories. He walked toward her, emerging from the bushes and leading an obese brown horse saddled English style. Sr. Inez thumped along by his side. Bodey dropped the reins and crossed the clearing until he stood within a foot of the woman he loved.

"Eve." He beseeched her to answer him.

"Bodey!" she exclaimed, backing away and nearly tripping over Sr. Helen who feebly pushed her back in Bodey's direction.

"We think you two need to duke it out, verbally, that is," Sr. Nessy said. "Get to it. Sr. Helen and I will be praying for you both on the other side of the shrine. We won't hear a thing."

As the elderly nuns shuffled to the far side of the shrine, Bodey tried to take Eve's hands, tried to gaze deeply into her misty gray eyes like a teenager smitten with a pretty girl. Eve slapped his hands away. The fight was on.

"You didn't answer my letters. Six, I wrote six. In

the first, I asked you to explain whatever you were talking about just before I left. In the second and third, I told you what I was doing and asked about your cows. In the fourth, I said I was getting uncomfortable with the situation on the island. In the fifth, I wrote you about coming back home. The sixth one said I never wanted to see you again, but I never mailed it because that contained a lie. I need to understand what happened to us, Bodey." Eve flushed with anger across her cheekbones. If she'd had a riding crop he'd be in for a hiding.

"Whoa, hold up! First of all, everyone in Rainbow is running around with enough postcards from you to make up a deck of cards, and I don't rate one note because none came for me. Your daddy made it pretty clear a cowboy wasn't good enough for his daughter, and the ring I had made up special for you wasn't worth nothin' because it didn't have some big honkin' diamond in it. He wanted you to marry royalty, and you went off with him, so I guessed that's what you wanted, too. I traveled to the islands to find you. Your father saw through my disguise and pitched me overboard before we reached his island. Good thing I wore sandals and not my boots, or I might not have made it back to shore. Your daddy tell you that? No? You ask Rusty. He came with me, dove overboard to make sure I didn't drown."

Eve's glance turned from accusatory to baffled. "You wore sandals. I've never seen you in anything but boots even on Sundays."

"I dressed up like an A-rab prince in one of those dresses and headpieces they wear to fool your father since he wanted you to marry one."

Eve pressed a hand to her pink lips to cover a small smile. "I would have loved to have seen that. But Bodey, your Texas accent—how did you expect to get away with it?"

"I pretended I didn't speak much English. Rusty posed as my interpreter. It worked pretty well until your dad saw my white ass when the wind blew my throbe nearly over my head."

From behind the shrine, a chorus of soft laughter sounded. Eve let loose with a chuckle, only one, but a good start toward forgiveness he figured.

"Look, if you like the idea, I can get another costume and an all-over tan. We can play..." He was stopped by Eve's suddenly grim expression and the recall of nuns listening in even if they claimed to be praying.

"No thanks. I recall another person with an all-over tan. Were you and Renee sunbathing together when I knocked at your door?"

"Hell, no. The light would of hurt my eyes too bad. Honest, I can't remember being with Renee in what they call the Biblical sense at all. Listen, as for those dozen kids you want, I'm willin' to give that a try, but it seems like extreme family planning to me. I figure we should have one or two like Noreen and Rusty to see how it goes, but if you don't want to practice birth control on account of your religion, that's fine by me. There, I'm done." Bodey took a deep breath.

"Whoever said I want a dozen children? I might be Catholic, but I'm not out of my mind," Eve said, grabbing at the last statement first, too distressed to mention Renee again.

Sr. Helen peeked around the shrine. "Ah, that

might have been our fault. You see, Sr. Nessy and I were testing Evan Adams' sincerity. That dozen figure just popped out during our conversation with the man. We can't imagine how it got back to Bodey."

"That's a relief. I was thinkin' two or three at the most," Bodey responded with a grin. "Not that I couldn't give you twelve of course."

Sr. Inez poked her head out from behind the side of the shrine closest to Eve. "Where did you mail your letters, dear? There must be a logical explanation," she said in a stage whisper.

"Daddy. Dad said to put my letters in with his business mail. He'd see they got where they belonged."

"The wastebasket, most likely, but you could have phoned or e-mailed. I got a web site, you know, where my fans can leave messages," Bodey said stubbornly.

"Right now, I'm not a big fan of yours. Besides, Dad is paranoid about my using the phone to call friends or do e-mail on his office computer. He is sure the IRS has been watching me all these years and waiting to pounce on him. That doesn't explain why you didn't contact *me* through *my* web site."

"You have a web site? Never thought of you as the computer geek type is all."

"No more than you. I display my art and refer customers and galleries to my site," she answered in a snippy tone.

"That's great, darlin'. Now that we've figured out how we lost each other for nearly three months, are we ready to stop talkin' and make up?" Bodey asked hopefully.

"Not hardly, Bodey Landrum. I'm gone barely three months, and I come home to find you having drunken orgies with Renee Hayes."

The voices murmuring prayers behind the shrine grew louder.

"One drunken orgy, just one! I was tryin' to get over you, Eve. Besides, how do I know you weren't sleeping around with sheiks and royalty the whole time you were gone, Miss Fancy Pants?"

"Don't you call me that! Sheiks and princes again! Are you out of your mind? Daddy did try to push me at every rich client who came to catch a swordfish. When he said he had another Arab client, I refused to go along on the boat. Must have been you because he said they only caught little fish that day."

"If you had been on that boat, I'd have thrown off those robes and taken you right there on the deck I would have been so happy to see you." Oops, he'd forgotten about the nuns again.

A small gasp escaped from one of the audience—probably Sr. Helen as Sr. Nessy, used to dealing with horses, didn't shock as easily and used some salty language herself.

Eve blushed, knowing they had overheard despite the murmured prayers. "With my father pushing me at rich men, it got so bad I moved out of his place in the end. You think you know me so well, Bodey Landrum—but you don't know I wouldn't sleep with a man if I didn't believe I loved him."

"So you do love me, honey!" Bodey opened his arms.

Eve didn't run into them. She kicked a pile of pine needles in his direction, folded her arms, and said, "Renee Hayes."

"I admit the woman slept in my bed, but I can't

remember havin' fuc—fornicated with her. I know evidence got scattered all over the place, but here in my heart, I know I didn't touch her. Darlin', you got to make a leap of faith about this." Bodey pounded his chest twice with a closed fist and gave Eve his best blue-eyed gaze. What else could he say to convince her?

"Eve, darlin', I think we must be soul mates 'cause I don't want any woman but you." Thank you, Noreen. If one cowboy could marry an Academy girl, why couldn't another?

"Renee wore my ring. I knew it was meant for me the second I saw it on her finger. Wisteria."

"Wisteria?" one of the nun's murmured.

Eve's gray eyes darkened. The shade reminded him of the times he laid with her. Hope grew. "Now, that I'm clear on. I kept the ring in a container by my bed. Renee helped herself."

He searched a pocket, found the ring, and held it out to Eve. She didn't move. She didn't speak. Something more was called for, something better than a proposal next to a dumpster or an offer during an argument. Think, Bodey, think.

He dropped to his knees in the pine needles. "Eve, accept this ring, and be my wife, my love, my soul mate."

Eve held out her hand, and Bodey slipped the amethyst on to the white finger of his convent rose where it belonged. A small sigh and a hoarse whisper came from behind the shrine. "Now!"

"Huh?" Bodey disregarded the pain of the pine needles probing through the fabric of his jeans, still kneeling, and still holding Eve's hand.

A shrill whistle came from the other side of the shrine. Brownie stopped cropping the Academy's shrubs, picked up his feet, and trotted toward the couple. An age-spotted hand slipped him a quarter of an apple. The drool of a happy horse dripped from his muzzle.

Bodey got to his feet. "Will you ride into the sunset with me, Eve?" Then, he eyed the short stirrups and tiny English saddle strapped on the bulging horse.

"I will, Bodey." Eve raised her eyebrows. "Want me to drive? Give me a leg up."

He tossed her into the saddle and pulled himself up behind. Eve kicked Brownie into a trot and began posting right up against him. Bodey Landrum rode into the sunset a happy man.

The two nuns watched the couple ride toward the west in the direction of the Three B's Ranch.

"Would you look at that sunset? Orange and Indian red, cadmium yellow, pink and turquoise. It's as pretty a rainbow," Sr. Helen said.

"God's own miracle, and it happens every day," Sr. Inez replied as the horse and riders passed out of sight over the crest of the hill.

Chapter Twenty-Three

All Bodey asked of Eve was that the wedding be a simple affair. He'd pay for anything she wanted, anywhere she desired, but please, not a lot of froufrou stuff like tuxedos with ruffled shirts and embroidered vests. All Eve asked of Bodey, and she asked quite a bit from him, was that her father be present. That meant an island wedding.

Bodey stuck to his guns and wore a pale gray suit with his bolo tie, a dress Stetson, and a pair of new lizard boots. In his opinion, everyone else except Eve and the two nuns in their short habits looked ridiculous draped in the wild floral prints Ja'nae Plato found in a boutique near the docks. He had to suppress a laugh every time he looked at Rusty holding the groom's Stetson and the two platinum wedding bands engraved with wisteria leaves. The red parrots and yellow flowers on his best man's shirt clashed with Rusty's hair something awful. White pants—the women had gotten Russ to wear white pants and sandals. And Leon Plato, why he resembled a calypso king with his balding head shaved down to the skin instead of an accountant. He only needed to add a gold earring.

Needless to say, Renee Niles Bouchard Hayes had not been invited to the wedding, though she would have rocked the bridesmaids' sarong-style dresses. Rusty's boy, Jesse, grudgingly carried the rings, a girly job he said. Little Katie joyously scattered white rose petals in their path. The big floral print wasn't too kind to Noreen's hips as she came down the aisle. In fact, the only one who looked really fine was Ja'nae which figured seeing as how she'd picked the costumes. Then, Eve appeared on her father's arm in the doorway of the small Catholic chapel surrounded by banana trees and took his breath away just as she always did.

She wore a simple long white dress tied behind her neck and a single red hibiscus blossom in her unbound hair. Eve encased her long toes in flat, golden sandals, careful not to be taller than Bodey. She held a spray of bird-of-paradise flowers in the crook of one arm and a crystal rosary and small, white Bible, gifts from Srs. Helen and Inez, in the other hand. Noreen took these items from the bride at the altar and Ja'nae held the bouquet. He and Eve exchanged traditional vows unmarred by bad poetry or awkward letters to each other and placed the rings on their fingers. The length of their kiss was simply embarrassing, Rusty claimed later.

Let the party begin! All who truly mattered had come to celebrate the unlikely union of the rodeo king and the convent rose except for Mama Tyne. Refusing to get on the charter flight, she claimed that puny little plane couldn't hold her up. She needed a whole 747 to herself. She did promise the finest reception Rainbow had ever seen after the couple returned home. Bodey's aunt and grandmother attended supplying the tears and his nieces the radiant smiles, even if they didn't bring barbeque with them. All his female relatives offered to watch Jesse and Katie so Noreen and Rusty could have a true Caribbean vacation. They were that kind of good people, and Bodey was proud of them.

Still, old Rich hadn't done badly in the food and drink department, offering trays of coconut shrimp and jerk chicken wings and an open bar with imported beers and endless varieties of beach drinks sporting paper parasols and chunks of fruit. A pink drink in one hand, Ja'nae swung her slim hips to the rhythm of the Caribbean band while she beckoned to any of the men to come dance with her.

Patrick O'Shea, not able to dance, shook hands with Rich Kuhl. He knew better than to ask about the surname since neither of their children bore their father's name, a topic to let ride. The bride and groom made the rounds, and Eve bent over Pat's wheelchair so he could kiss the bride.

Her own father gave her a hug and said with tears in his eyes, "I always thought you'd be married in the cathedral, baby, with a dozen bridesmaids and a dress fit for a princess."

"It's not the place or the dress that counts, Dad. It's the man. I got the real deal, you know."

"But, Eve, a cowboy?"

"What's wrong with that?" asked Pat, his usually merry blue eyes turning hard and a fist bunching on the arm of his wheelchair as if he would take on Rich Kuhl right here, right now. Man, having a daddy come to your defense was great. Bodey almost teared up himself.

Backing off, arms in the air, Rich went to bump hips with Ja'nae and gradually warmed to his son-in-law as the champagne made the rounds. "You say you made a few million riding bulls?"

"That and the endorsements and the investments. It

adds up."

"You see, son, I'm a little overextended. Those last two boats, well, I shouldn't have expanded so soon. Ever consider investing in a charter fishing operation?"

"It's been my dream," Bodey said and wrote the check. He figured he'd own the fleet in the next few years and probably the whole private island—a nice place to take their future kids for vacation.

As the tropical sun set, torches lit the scene and the party continued far into the night, but without the bride and groom who had slipped away to a suite at the Ritz-Carlton to celebrate their wedding night. Bodey and Eve watched the last rays fade into the ocean from their private balcony.

"It ain't no prettier than the one at the Academy the day you rode off with me," Bodey said.

"No, that sunset will always be my favorite. Come to bed, Bodey."

Eve went in first but didn't fuss with fancy nightwear. She simply untied the straps around her neck, slid down the short zipper at her back, and let the white dress fall. Clad in only a pair of lace panties and her golden sandals, she waited for her groom. After a moment's appreciation, he relieved her of those items and laid her on the bed.

"Condom?" he asked out of consideration for his bride.

"No, I want you to feel all that I feel. We don't need to use them anymore."

"No argument from me, my convent rose. I don't think your feelings for me are all tangled up like wisteria anymore, and you just proved you ain't a Miss Fancy Pants by marryin' me. I kind of like the idea that

I stole you from the nuns."

"I believe the Blessed Mother Leontine gave me to you."

"Whatever you want to believe so long as we are together." Bodey mounted up for a long, slow, pleasurable ride home.

Epilogue

Children did come to Bodey and Eve, the first boy nine months after the wedding ceremony, another son twelve months later, and a third eighteen months after that. Thrilled as they were with Shea Patrick, Benjamin Barnum, and Richard Russell, Eve and Bodey concluded natural family planning didn't work well for a couple who enjoyed each other as much as they did. They decided mutually they'd reached their limit with the three boys. Eve made sure they attended church every Sunday to thank God and Mother Leontine for their blessings.

As for the town of Rainbow, the village prospered in a small way, though art was never its main commodity. Young women continued to be educated there in godly ways and achieved strong character. People came to see the famous Academy and visit the grave of the Blessed Mother Leontine to pray for her guidance and to grant them special favors. Some stayed to experience spiritual renewal behind its gates. Like the marriage of a cowboy to an Academy girl, small miracles so commonplace as to be barely noticeable continued to occur quite regularly.

Is Renee Niles Bouchard Hayes worthy of true love? Find out in A WILD RED ROSE.

A word about the author...

Once a librarian, now a writer of romance, Lynn Shurr grew up in Pennsylvania Dutch country. She attended a state college and earned a very impractical degree in English Literature. Her first job out of school really was working in a burger joint. Moving from one humble job to another, she finally buckled down and studied for an M.A. in Librarianship.

She found her first reference job in the Heart of Cajun Country. For her, the old saying, "Once you've tasted bayou water, you will always stay here" came true. She raised three children not far from the Bayou Teche and lives there still with her astronomer husband.

When not writing, Lynn likes to paint, cheer for the New Orleans Saints and LSU Tigers, and take long road trips nearly anywhere. Her love of the bayou country, its history and customs, often shows in the background of her books.

You may contact Lynn at www.lynnshurr.com or visit her personal blog: lynnshurr.blogspot.com.

She is also a regular contributor to:

www.romancingthejock.com

Thank you for purchasing
this publication of The Wild Rose Press, Inc.
For other wonderful stories of romance,
please visit our on-line bookstore at
www.thewildrosepress.com.

For questions or more information
contact us at
info@thewildrosepress.com.

The Wild Rose Press, Inc.
www.thewildrosepress.com

To visit with authors of
The Wild Rose Press, Inc.
join our yahoo loop at
http://groups.yahoo.com/group/thewildrosepress/

www.ingramcontent.com/pod-product-compliance
Lightning Source LLC
Chambersburg PA
CBHW070913180626
46817CB00003B/1036